What do you do when you think you've found the most wonderful guy? Except maybe he isn't?

When Montgomery Monty Pellman meets Sawyer on Rodeo Drive in Beverly Hills, he's ecstatic to connect with somebody who isn't a weirdo or some fly-by-night straight, married guy on the down-low on Grindr.

Sawyer is everything he's ever wanted and more. Blistering-hot sex and brilliant conversation lead to Monty impulsively inviting him to Thanksgiving dinner. Sawyer seems thrilled, but then creepy things start happening. Monty is sure Sawyer is stalking him, and the guy strongly resembles a serial killer on the loose in Los Angeles.

Sawyer is obsessed with Monty. He has been for many years, not that he can tell him this. He knows the truth will make the guy run. He needs Monty to fall in love with him to break an old curse, and he has just one week to do it.

That's if he survives Monty's family's bizarre southern Thanksgiving meal complete with his Grammy's pickles in gelatin and her crazy Coke salad.

Kill the Moon
Copyright © 2020 A.J. Llewellyn
ISBN: 978-1-4874-3158-7
Cover art by Martine Jardin

Published by eXtasy Books Inc or
Devine Destinies, an imprint of eXtasy Books Inc

Look for us online at:
www.eXtasybooks.com or www.devinedestinies.com

KILL THE MOON

BY

A.J. LLEWELLYN

DEDICATION

To Bob Ryan

And

To all those who believe in life after love

When it's gone, you'll know what a gift love was. You'll suffer like this. So, go back and fight to keep it.

— Ian McEwan

CHAPTER ONE

M onty approached the line of people standing outside the Louis Vuitton store on Rodeo Drive in Beverly Hills. He tried to remember everything his handler had emailed him and focused his efforts on not locking gazes with anyone else waiting.

It was hard. Very hard.

The dark-haired man with the electric blue eyes was just too damned handsome.

And, oh, gulp. He's looking at me. He's looking at me! Monty tried not to slam into the velvet-roped stanchions separating the crowd from the store. Now he wanted to laugh as he got into line three people behind the blue-eyed hunk. Had anyone else realized how ridiculous it was that they were loitering outside an open but completely empty store?

He understood that with California's lingering pandemic laws, safe social distancing was still the rule of the land. But sheesh. Nobody was in the shop. Not a single customer. He tugged at the elastic straps of his face mask. He'd been warned Beverly Hills was rigorous about the damned things. The cops were swift to ticket you if you didn't wear one, even on the street. His new cloth mask itched his freshly shaved chin.

His gaze fell to the expensive-looking decals on every square of paving on the sidewalk, screaming at people to keep six feet between them. With a jolt, he stepped back and earned a yelp of anguish from a woman behind him.

Monty turned. "I'm so sorry!"

The raven-haired Goth-looking beauty waved off his apology and rubbed her foot with the other. She texted frantically on her cell phone with one hand and sipped at a Nespresso cup with the other. *Dexterous.*

Monty glanced forward again and locked glances with the hunk, who had turned to look at him. Oh, boy, he was delicious. Monty approved of his black pants, white shirt, and leather jacket ensemble. Sexy as hell.

After months of quick showers, no shaving, and rotating the same three pairs of shorts and t-shirts, Monty had spruced himself up for today. He'd even borrowed his mom's mango and ginger shampoo. *I smell like a fruit tree.* He glanced down and noticed his mismatched socks. *Oh, great. I look like I dressed in the dark. Black pants, black jeans, one orange sock and a brown one.*

He peered inside the massive windows that were so bright and sparkly they seemed like mirrors. A couple of store clerks rushed around, trying to look busy but weren't doing very much, a swipe of white fabric on a shelf here, adjusting a shoe there. They must have gotten the same memo because they wouldn't look at the people waiting for entry into the place.

Monty blew out a breath, and reflected in the window, he caught the gaze of the blue-eyed hunk once more. The guy even looked hot with a face mask on. He was smiling. Monty knew it because his eyes were crinkling above the edge of the mask. Monty smiled back, then averted his gaze. Seventeen people had now lined up outside the store. Not any other store on the street had anyone standing out front. In fact, the area was like a ghost town—a well-appointed, pricey ghost town.

Rodeo Drive was the richest street in the world, and it contained the most expensive menswear store in the known galaxy. Monty would never understand its appeal. The House of Bijan bedazzled rich and poor folk alike. He knew tourists had always flocked to Rodeo Drive to glimpse the store's legendary wares. Not an easy thing to do when this establishment could only be entered by appointment. Monty had never been impressed by Bijan's bizarre, freakish clothing. In his good days, his dad had enjoyed going in and being fussed over by a few assistants. But the good days were long gone.

Monty sighed. Not all of Bijan's stuff was weird, but every single item was way overpriced. He'd never met anyone who'd even *considered* purchasing a thirty-thousand-dollar crocodile skin-trimmed sweater or an eighteen-thousand-dollar cashmere pea coat.

His father had bought one sportscoat a year ago and rarely took it off, telling people, "Bijan, you know."

Monty was only surprised his father hadn't left the price tag on it as proof.

It was a good thing his dad, Montgomery *Monty* Pellman, Sr., had developed an unhealthy attachment to that one single sportscoat. Monty had learned the average Bijan customer spent near a quarter of a million dollars a year there.

He realized he was in no position to be a shopping snob since he was loitering outside another expensive store under false pretenses. But he wouldn't spend a dime . . . not one red cent.

The things I do for a hundred bucks. That made him curious about the hunk. *Why's he here? Is he hard up too?*

None of the stores that were open appeared to have any customers. The few people walking on the street threw curious glances at the cluster outside the Louis Vuitton store. The only place doing any real business was Nespresso. They'd removed almost all their tables out front, with respect for the six-foot rule, which left three small tables spaced far apart and filled with a few shoppers juggling phones and takeout cups. *I shoulda had a second cup of coffee before I came here.* Monty sighed. He'd lose his place in line if he went over to the coffee bar. People milled around inside, but the line also flowed out the door, which meant two stores were boasting some pretty good business.

"Okay," said a store clerk coming out to greet them. That was the only word Monty understood. Everything else behind the man's LV emblazoned mask came out muffled.

The woman behind Monty's voice rang clear. "What did he say?"

"No idea." Monty resisted the urge to laugh.

He caught her gaze, and she seemed to be fighting the desire too. Some of the people at the head of the line went inside the store. That left a woman in a frilly 1940s dress, which appeared to be made of vintage curtain fabric, the hunk, two people busy taking selfies, Monty, and a stack of people behind him. He counted five shoppers in the store. How long would he have to be out here?

When he applied for the job of being a fake shopper, he did it on a whim. And who couldn't use an easy hundred bucks these days? The man, who hired him over the phone, told him he'd have to stay in line, take a selfie of himself, then one more in the store with some product, and post these to Instagram, Snapchat, and Facebook. Twitter apparently didn't count.

The woman behind Monty nudged him. "Wanna be in my selfie?"

"Sure. If I can get one with you, too."

He got his camera ready, and they snapped off shots. She smelled of a faint, tantalizing perfume. He couldn't identify it and had to give up the mental foot chase as the line lurched forward.

"My name is Lucille," the woman said. "Lucille Ball."

Monty got busy uploading his photo to his social media sites. He posted to Twitter for the heck of it. "Is that your real name?"

"No. I changed it."

Monty paused in his posting. "How's that working out for

you?"

By the way Lucille's already taut mask pulled at the sides, she was grinning. "Well enough for me to be a fake shopper. Ooh, look, the line's moving again."

They shuffled forward. As a few customers came back outside, six others were allowed inside.

"Nobody's buying anything," a male sales associate whispered in such a dramatic stage whisper they would have heard him on Broadway. If Broadway shows had been back in business.

Monty's employer had assured him that he didn't need to buy anything. As he and Lucille made their way inside, he kept his gaze on a wall display of suitcases that seemed suspended in midair. It was a clever effect.

Lucille tapped Monty's shoulder. "You haven't told me your name."

"Sorry. Monty Pellman."

She threw her hands into the air. "Oh, my God. I *knew* it. You're him!" Her shriek seemed to attract everyone's attention. "You're the cheese guy!"

Monty blew out a breath. "That's me."

"You have that fantastic cheese. The one with the live maggots!"

"No, I don't." *Oh, man, did the hunk hear her?*

A few people in the store were staring at him now — including the hunk. Maggots had a way of drawing unwanted attention.

"Yeah, you do. You're the cheese guy." Lucille waggled a finger at him.

Monty winced. "Yes, but we don't sell that cheese anymore. Customs banned it."

Her eyes took on a slight droop above her mask. "That's so sad. I was at the bridal shower where you and your dad served it. Those maggots tasted so good! He's awesome, by the way. Cute as a bug. How is he these days?"

Cute? What is she smoking? "He's fine." He didn't mean to snap at her, but he could tell the hunk was listening. He didn't want to have to explain about the maggots. He took a deep sigh. People always wanted to ask about the maggots. And eat them.

She flapped a hand at him. "He's adorable. I saw you at that cheese and wine festival up in Santa Rosa. When was it?" She put a fingertip coated in black lacquer to her mask. "June last year."

"Yep. That was us."

"I'm in costume."

Did she mean she was wearing a costume, or she worked in the costume business?

"I work for Western Costume," she said. "I also work as a Lucille Ball lookalike."

She looked nothing like Lucy. "What do you do about the hair? She was a redhead."

"Wigs." She scrolled through her phone and showed him a photo.

He was surprised to see she really did look like Lucy. Amazing what good makeup could do.

"Could you and your dad cater my bridal shower? You did that one for my friend. She's still talking about it. Give me your number. I'll call and set it up." She dropped her voice. "I'd love it if you could bring the maggoty cheese."

Monty gave her his cell phone number. *When did we last do a bridal shower?* He felt the ever-present ache in his heart and gut squeeze him just a little bit. It was hard to talk about his dad and the devastating effects the coronavirus lockdown had on their cheese shop right around the corner on Brighton Way.

"When are you getting married?" he asked, just to show interest.

She waved a hand around in a breezy way. "No idea. I'm still single and ready to mingle. But you never know, do you? Are you straight?"

"Um—"

"No." She interrupted him with a sigh. "I thought not. You're too nice to be straight. Oh, look at that pink hat on that display shelf. Too cool for school."

Monty let her lean past him even though she was violating safe social distancing rules. He was too busy thinking about his dad, in a wilderness of his own in an assisted living facility for Alzheimer's patients. Monty's mother was still living in the family home but not coping with the lockdown at all. She hadn't left the house since March seventeenth, the day California went into statewide closure.

Monty hated visiting his dad. Losing his mind meant his dad often forgot to ask how the shop was doing. Lately, his dad even started saying he hated cheese.

Lucille took lots of photos. "I loved the demonstration you did with the Japanese cheeses. I can still taste those cherries."

Japanese. That bridal shower would have been two years ago. His dad had personally traveled to Hokkaidō and returned with a shipment of *sakura*—cherry blossom—cheese. Monty wondered if he would ever be able to get it back in the store again. It was the most delicate, delicious thing he'd ever eaten in his life. Flavored with the leaves of the succulent mountain cherry, it had a smooth, creamy texture, unlike anything he'd ever tasted.

Thanks to the pandemic, however, it was impossible to import cheese from just about anywhere. His expensive, well-kept varieties had been destroyed, thanks to riot and looting back in June, which had spread from downtown LA to the Valley. His refrigerators had been damaged. Some cheeses were stolen, the rest trashed by thugs. All his branded cookware, hats, mugs—almost all of it gone. He'd had to start all over again. Now his store stood empty and clean — beyond clean. He'd passed the city's safety inspection and hoped to be up and running with a small selection of products in time for Thanksgiving in eight days and in full steam by Christmas next month.

It really seemed, however, that it would be the New Year before he was fully operational again. He wouldn't be allowed to have indoor tables for customers purchasing quick snacks and coffee. He relied on that extra trade for the tips. He sighed. His loyal staff of two had been getting unemployment. Rima, his pastry chef who did wonders with his soft cheeses, was now giving free online classes out of her own kitchen. It had bothered Monty at first because many of the recipes she shared were his. Actually, old family recipes handed down to him from his paternal great Grammy's side of the family. *Good thing Dad's out of his mind. Otherwise, he'd insist we sue her.*

Monty took a deep breath and once again tried not to stress. He was happy she'd found a way to keep busy doing the job she loved. *I wish she'd just asked me if it was okay to give out those recipes.* He was still torn on whether to bring her back because of it. If he did, Rima would have to sign a nondisclosure agreement, particularly with the holidays coming up. He had plans to include super-secret recipes handed down from his Southern ancestors — unusual classics like cheese coins in the mix. It would be awful if she took all of those, too.

On the other hand, the customers loved her and the way she made sweet cheese rolls and hot pepper cream cheese Danishes.

Like Monty, she and Laurent, his only other permanent employee, had made unwelcome dents in their savings. The crush of his financial burdens weighed on him. His father hadn't been in good shape for a long time, but until he'd fallen and hit his head in March, he'd gone to work daily. His father's decline had been swift and frightening.

I can't think about him now. At least he's in a good, safe place, and they're taking care of him.

Monty had hoped to have his dad as well as Rima and Laurent back working with him. But Laurent, his best salesman, had wigged out and gone camping up the California coast. He posted strange photos of himself with his dog daily, outside rustic wooden cabins up and down the rugged highway, and his middle finger pointed at the camera.

I know how he feels. Monty fiddled with the price tag on a bright pink shirt. For some reason, it appealed to him, but not his wallet. Seventeen hundred and fifty dollars. Pink seemed to be the hot color for Louis Vuitton. Monty glanced up the stairs of the cavernous space and paused in his mental meanderings. He couldn't remember the last time he'd bought clothes . . . or anything not related to work.

He'd scheduled a meeting for the next day with a cheese distributor from LA's downtown market district with a direct line to French cheese imports. The guy had promised to *dazzle* him with his new line of products.

I know I have to spend money to make money. But not on shirts. Monty moved on to another rack of tops and pants. He liked to joke with Rima that he had about six months before he'd have to consider panhandling on the edge of the freeway. *Stop freaking yourself out, idiot.* It wasn't that he was almost destitute. He'd kept up his mortgage payments and all his other commitments for seven months now without any income. Federal reimbursement had finally kicked in four months into the pandemic, but like many other Americans, the uncertainty of it all scared the heck out of him. He made a show of studying the beautiful but useless items he'd never buy, even if he had the spare funds.

Will we ever get through this? He wandered through the store, checking price tags, and took a photo of himself with Lucille. His gaze fell on a mink hat that just broke his heart. *How many animals died to make this monstrosity?* The three-thousand-dollar price tag almost sent him into despair.

"I'm your biggest fan." Lucille plonked a hideous, see-through canary yellow rainhat with LV stamped all over it on his head and took a photo of him.

"Really? Why?" Monty couldn't understand it.

One of the clerks rushed over and yanked it off again. "You can't try on things and not buy them. Coronavirus, baby."

Lucille ignored him, posting her photo to the Internet. "I'm crazy about cheese, cheese guy. I saw the sign on your window as I came over here. You're re-opening tomorrow! I can't wait. You know which cheese I love, don't you?"

Monty hesitated. He'd never seen her before today, so how could he know? She'd mentioned the cheese he hated, and a wave of something unpleasant washed over him, and in that moment, he knew. *Oh, no. She's gonna turn out to be one of those* . . . He often found that cheese fans expected him to intuitively know their favorite varieties, as though he was some kind of psychic to the dairy industry.

"I adore *Milbenkäse*."

Was she for real? The German cheese was so revolting he would never get the smell out of his brain, and it had been years since he'd been near it. "You like cheese that's been fermented by cheese mites?" Milbenkäse smelled like pooh. Which was what encased it. Insect pooh.

Lucille grabbed his shoulder. "Yes! And that sour smell. Wow. Nothing like it. But thanks to you, *Casu marzu* is my real favorite. I'm obsessed."

Her dramatic tone almost made him run. Her hand seemed cold. Freezing. It sent strange icy tendrils of fear down his body. The sensation took his breath away. He took a step back as images of ice filled his mind. *Why oh, why does she keep going on about that disgusting cheese?*

But she was smiling. "I can't believe I'm saying this, but I miss maggots."

Eeeww! Monty shook his head. He couldn't say the same

thing. His father had forced him to try the Casu marzu when they first brought it to LA a few years ago. Once the true nature of the live-maggot-infested cheese was made public, He and his dad had been forbidden to import any more of it from Sardinia.

He gulped. "I have a hard time eating anything that moves."

Lucille flapped a delicate hand. "Oh, but those maggots were *amazing*. That cheese was so stinky but so awesome. You know your maggots."

"No, I don't."

"You don't?" She looked crushed. "I'm so bummed. I love that velvety rich taste of those little critters. Kinda like sour cream and a hint of black pepper."

I think I'm gonna barf.

"Do any of your other cheeses come with them?"

"Certainly not!"

She looked so disappointed it made him laugh. She was a bit of a nut, but he liked her. He'd become aware of the hunk's scrutiny and busied himself checking the price on the ridiculous rainhat. *Eleven hundred dollars. Now I've seen everything.*

"Are you going to buy it?" The salesclerk's nose twitched like an irritated rabbit.

"I don't think so, no." Monty gave him a smile, and his own nose began doing weird things. Coffee. *Why do I smell fresh coffee?*

"Here. Try this. You look like you could use it." The hunk's voice tickled Monty's ear like water gently rippling over a book.

"Thanks." He took the small cup emblazoned with the Louis Vuitton initials and lowered his mask enough to take a sip, then pulled it back up again. The coffee was black. Not the way he liked it, but it was delicious and made him feel good. "I think I'll take a selfie." He positioned his camera, held up the cup, and snapped a shot, careful to include the hunk in it. "Can I tag you on it?" He turned, but the hunk had his back to him, talking to Lucille.

The hunk took a photo of himself with the bossy salesclerk. Monty had no idea why it bothered him so much, but it did. He posted his two store photos to his social media sites, then sent the required text to his employer. It took a few more minutes before he received a notification from Venmo that a private payment of a hundred dollars had been sent to his account. He was free to leave.

Monty turned to find the hunk staring at him.

"The lovely Lucille and I are going to have lunch at my place. I have an outdoor terrace. I thought we'd order food from Caffé Roma." He paused for a fraction of a second. "My treat."

"I adore the Roma. I . . . sure." Monty smiled wide, feeling buoyant for the first time in months.

"Do you know the menu?" The hunk turned his phone toward Monty.

"I sort of do. I like their salads and pastas. But um, I really love their Americano pizza."

The hunk's infectious laughter rang out as the three of them made it outside the store, allowing another small group to shuffle their way inside.

"Lucille, our friend here likes Roma's Americano pizza." The hunk focused his gaze on her.

"I adore pizza. It just doesn't adore me." She ran her hands down her svelte figure. "What's on an Americano, anyway?"

"Mozzarella cheese, tomato sauce, sausage, and French fries." Monty waited for her to react. Most people gagged at the mention of fries on a pizza.

She surprised him by saying, "Sounds groovy. I'm down with that. We'd better get a couple of salads too."

"Gotcha." The hunk smiled at Monty. "I'm Sawyer, by the way."

Monty grinned back. *Sawyer*. What a sexy name. Over the next few minutes, the small group picked out their pizza and salad options, and wandered up to the restaurant, pausing to window-shop on the way. Lucille wanted a coffee, so they stopped at Nespresso, where they purchased small cups. It was so nice that some niceties in life had been returned to civilized people in these troubled times.

Monty loved the smooth, rich Odacio blend he'd chosen for his brew but had to stop Sawyer from buying an entire sleeve of the pods for him. They made it to the restaurant over on Canon Drive several minutes later.

One of the waiters rushed over to Sawyer as they entered the leafy, arched pathway to the outdoor dining area.

"Mr. Sawyer, sir! We have your order ready." He beckoned him, Lucille, and Monty, toward a delivery table loaded with takeout orders bagged and awaiting pickup, gigantic bottles of hand sanitizer, and a collection of paper masks.

Sawyer nodded. "Thank you, Joe. It all smells fantastic." He slid the guy a twenty-dollar bill.

That surprised Monty, but then again, it didn't. A lot of people were over tipping these days because the last several months had been so difficult for everyone.

Salad days are here again! Monty blinked. Now, what the hell did that expression mean, and why had it popped into his head?

"Oh, thank you, sir, Mr. Sawyer." Joe looked genuinely ecstatic. He pointed a gloved hand at the takeout bags. "Here is your order. I packed extra bread and dipping oil because I know how much you enjoy that." He dropped his voice. "And some extra containers of our salad dressing."

"Good man. Thank you." Sawyer took hold of the bags and passed out a couple to Lucille and Monty. "Shall we?" He beamed at them from behind his mask.

"Sure. I'm starved." Lucille tossed back her long dark hair.

13

Monty wondered what on earth possessed her to change her name. *Wonder if Lucille's having a ball?* The question popped into his mind. *Geez, and I'm totally sober!*

They walked north along Rodeo Drive. People were out, but it wasn't the usual mind-boggling cluster of tourists. A rugged-looking man in shorts and flipflops passed them, clutching shopping bags from Malibu Clothing. Despite his unkempt appearance, he must have had money because Malibu Clothing was another appointment-only store. He muttered in Farsi into his cell phone. Monty recognized it because it was the second language in Beverly Hills.

He picked out the word, *Khoobam*, which meant, *I'm doing well.*

We've all gotten used to listening to muffled voices on phones. Man. Monty felt a pang of guilt. *I should call Mom and warn her I'll be late. She worries about everything, from drones to traffic jams.*

At a stoplight on Little Santa Monica Boulevard, they waited to cross the road. Monty squashed his paper cup and tossed it into a bin. A homeless man pounced on it. Before Monty could reach into his wallet to give the guy a few bills, Sawyer handed the guy a twenty. *Wow, he's so nice.* The light took forever to change, but it gave Monty the time to send his mom a text.

Having a quick bite, don't worry. I'm fine. Be home soon.

She texted back, *Bring milk.*

He sent her a smiley emoji, and she sent back three. His mom was into everything electronic, which amazed him. He felt better about taking a little time away from her. Frankly, being a fake shopper had been a good reason to get out of the house. She'd been so odd lately. There had been the epic fits of strange redecorating, painting, and always muttering, *Out with the blue!* She pored over old family photos that she would hide the second he came into the room.

"It has to be done right," she would say as though it explained everything. "Don't you see? A terrible wrong was done. And I'm sorry, sweetheart. I am so sorry."

He worried she was going off the Alzheimer's cliff, too. And he couldn't bear the thought. That would leave him with only his Grammy, who stood on the porch night and day, staring out at the neighborhood mumbling things in her weird, complicated language. She'd been a Southern girl, a beautiful mix of Gullah — West Indian descent born in South Carolina's Beaufort Sea Islands — and white American. Monty had never been to the family home in South Carolina. His mom had whispered it was filled with bad luck. Dad would never talk about it.

And Grammy would only say, "One day, the truth will out."

And in the meantime, she cooked.

He trotted along with Lucille and Sawyer until they reached Carmelita Avenue and made a right turn. It was a beautiful street with wide, emerald green lawns and houses set away from the road. Monty liked Carmelita because the homes, though Beverly Hills-huge, were not as ostentatious as some of the others in the neighborhood.

On the corner of a pristine laneway, Sawyer said, "This is it."

Relief surged through Monty, who was starving. His stomach rumbled, and it took everything in him not to dive into the shopping bag he was carrying to pull out a bread roll, anything, to get him through the next few minutes.

The house was set far back from the road, with majestic magnolias decorating the front of the property. Their faint smell reminded him of . . . what exactly? Nostalgia hit his senses, but he didn't know why.

Nobody said a word as they entered the quiet, cool place. Monty liked the big, sprawling ranch-style house painted white with plantation shutters decorating the windows that had been painted brown. And recently too, he was certain.

Sawyer led them inside, and all three of them removed their masks. Monty hated the masks but knew they were necessary. The house was big but had little decoration. Sawyer caught his flickering gaze.

"I moved in a couple of weeks ago."

Monty nodded. He didn't see boxes anywhere but figured the guy was nothing like him. *I'm a hoarder in training.* He grinned at the thought of what he would ever do without his books and vintage record collection.

Sawyer and Lucille kept up a repertoire about plates and glasses, and between them all, they managed to get outside with the food bags and the stuff they'd need to eat with a little grace.

The backyard was pretty. More trees and small bushes decorated the lawn. It felt unreal, though, sort of temporary. They set the bags down on a beautiful farmhouse style table, which could have been a genuine Southern relic, or maybe Pier 1. *Why do I care where he bought his stuff? What the hell is wrong with me?* He moved into one of the cushioned chairs opposite Lucille. When Sawyer slipped back into the house, Lucille took the opportunity to reach across the table and pat Monty's hand.

"I think he likes you."

Monty noticed for the first time her lips had shiny black gloss on them. *I didn't know women wore lipstick under their face masks. Doesn't it stain?*

"I like him too," he said and opened the bag beside him.

Sawyer returned with a pitcher of liquid that was bright green and smelled like mint.

"Iced tea." He poured it into the three glasses. "Made from an old family recipe."

"Thank you." Monty was about to sip when Lucille held up her glass.

"May we all one day be old friends." She clinked her glass to theirs with such force, Monty was afraid they'd shatter. But still, it was a wonderful sentiment. Almost as perfect as the iced mint tea.

"Oh." Monty moaned. "That's so good. What's in it?"

"Spearmint. Not peppermint. That's the secret. And there's another, but I won't tell." Sawyer chuckled. "I drink this stuff all day long."

"If I lived here, I would too," Monty said, then realized how it sounded. "I um, I er, don't mean —"

"I take it as a compliment." Sawyer raised his glass to him and took another drink. The guy seemed to take pleasure in the details. He commented on the spearmint leaves, the different food they ate, the tang of the dressing.

Monty had never met anyone so appreciative of the bounty before him. "Where's your family from?" he asked.

Sawyer stopped chewing for a moment. He seemed to glance at Lucille. "South Carolina," he said at last.

Monty was astonished. "So's my mom's family."

"Small world." Sawyer picked at the topping on his pizza slice.

"And how long have you been in LA?"

"Oh. A long time." Sawyer's face took on a closed expression. "Now. I couldn't help overhearing about you and cheese. With all the varieties you've probably ever eaten, I find it intriguing that you enjoy pizza with the least interesting version of it. Mozzarella."

"I adore mozzarella." Monty hoisted out his third slice of pizza. He hadn't been so happy in months. He could get used to hanging out with these two and eating gourmet takeout.

Suddenly, he remembered his cheese shop was still closed. He had no idea what to expect when he opened the following day. He'd work alone. He didn't expect it to be chaotic, judging by the way things looked in Beverly Hills today.

But I have no cheese. He brushed the thought aside. The cheese vendor would deliver the goods. *I should call and check everything's okay*. Would people come and buy his cheese once he was ready to roll? The uncertainty depressed him.

"I adore mozzarella too," Lucille said. "Even if it doesn't have maggots on it."

Sawyer wrinkled his nose. "Personally, I can live without maggots."

She shrugged, her eyes dancing with mischief. "More for me." She plucked a French fry from her pizza and ate it.

"Yeah. I never want to see maggots on anything near my mouth again." Monty touched his stomach. "I'm meeting a cheese merchant tomorrow from Paris. He says he has delicacies for me. He says he even has *Franche-Comté*, which the French consider the king of cheeses. I hope he's for real. The cheese world is full of . . ." He hunted for the right word. "Noodles."

"Noodles?" Lucille asked as she and Sawyer laughed.

Monty couldn't help laughing, too. He realized they'd worked their way through every bite of food before them.

Lucille smiled. "If you need help in the store, I'm a cheese wiz. I adore Franche-Comté. Truly one of my favorites." She waved an expressive hand again. "It's excellent in quiche, you know."

Monty knew the French prized that cheese in quiches and other savory pastries and planned to discuss the possibility with Rima.

She'd pooh-poohed the idea, insisting that just saying a quiche contained unusual, rare cheese was enough to make people buy it. "You could put Velveeta in it, and most people will think it's a gourmet dish."

Monty hadn't agreed with her. He didn't like lying about key ingredients in his food. Not that it was a real issue now. Rima had made it clear she didn't need him anymore.

"And anyway, I'm looking for a job." Lucille winked at him.

Monty had a feeling he'd be calling her soon. "Give me your number." He put it into his phone, and he was thrilled when he and Sawyer exchanged numbers, too.

"I'll be in touch." Sawyer gave him an enigmatic smile.

Monty wanted to dance like Michael Flatley. *Why am I so damned happy? I don't even know this man!*

Time stood still as Monty and Lucille rose to their feet.

"Leave it all," Sawyer instructed.

Monty didn't want to go home. He longed to stay. But he let Sawyer see him out of the house again. His cell phone buzzed. Mom.

Where are you? My coffee's gone cold.

Three hours had gone by. *How. Where?*

"I know this isn't socially safe, but I can't help myself." Sawyer stood at his back gate and put his arms around him.

Monty took a deep breath, loving the warmth and strength of the man holding him. He smelled so good — a little bit soap, a little bit pizza. There was a fragility, too, that surprised him. He returned the hug, shocked to the core when Sawyer's lips touched his ear.

"Kill the moon," he whispered.

CHAPTER TWO

K ill the moon. *What the hell is that supposed to mean?* Monty felt wobbly as he made his way back to his car, parked in the indoor public lot between Canon and Beverly Drives. He'd parked on the Beverly side, but his addled brain left him walking in circles for so long a security guard on a bicycle rode up to him.

"Lost your vehicle, sir?"

Monty grimaced, feeling stupid. "Sorry. I have my car alarm on here. I should have used it first." He clicked it, and the horn dutifully beeped at him from the other end of the aisle. "Thank you, though."

The security guard gave him a little wave and rode away again. Inside Monty's prized silver Ford Fiesta, the first brand-new vehicle he'd ever owned in his life, he cranked up the AC. He needed it. *What the hell is happening to me? It's been a week of weirdness. First Mom, now this.*

His breath caught at Adam Lambert's haunting version of *Believe.* For long moments, Monty gripped the steering wheel without moving. His life had been strange, he had to admit. There were times when nothing made sense, times when he never thought he'd find love. Real, lasting love. In this moment, for some reason, he believed in life after love being maybe . . . possible.

Still not moving, he gazed off into the middle distance. *Kill the moon.* It tickled his brain. *Why do I feel I should remember?* He thought it was somewhere in some long, lost, forgotten place. *No. It's not coming to me. What the hell was in that iced tea?*

His senses seemed heightened, but he wasn't drunk. Just super happy. And yes, confused.

Monty texted his mom and asked if she wanted anything else.

Shortbread cookies.

He texted back a thumbs up, and she sent a string of emojis, including one that looked like a birthday cake. She had a sweet tooth, that one.

Monty hated parking beyond the free two-hours given in Beverly Hills but didn't begrudge it this time. He kept thinking about lunch and how much he enjoyed Lucille and Sawyer. *I could swear they're old friends.* He shook the thought from his mind and handed the parking attendant his credit card. Once he made it out onto Canon, he turned right and headed east toward his mother's house in LA's Crestview neighborhood. An old suburb, it was lowkey enough to have escaped both becoming rundown or gentrified. His parents had owned the home for thirty-two years, two years before Monty was born.

He'd moved out twelve years ago and had spent most of that time back East. Two years ago, at his mom's insistence, he'd moved back to LA but had only moved into the house in the last few weeks. Things had been difficult before his dad had been put into assisted living. So far, Monty and his mom were getting along well.

He resisted renting out his condo in West Hollywood because it was his refuge when her obsessive-compulsive disorder kicked in, and she'd demand the oddest things. On the other hand, the extra income would be handy.

He made it to the Bevwood Market in the strip mall on South Robertson in record time, strolling the crowded aisles tossing things he knew she'd love into a hand cart. He stopped by Baskin Robbins on his way back to his car. He picked up pints of Cherries Jubilee and Jamoca Almond Fudge for her, and a cone with Caramel Turtle Truffle for himself. For some reason, he always craved sweets at the end of every meal.

Back behind the wheel, he was startled to see a vintage black sports car zoom past him. *Man! I think that's Lucille driving that thing!* He peeled out of the parking lot and followed the car. She was heading north toward the Hollywood Hills. *Where did she say she lived? I can't remember.* He loved classic cars, and as he switched lanes to get beside her, his gaze fixed on what he recognized now as a Karmann Ghia, circa 1972. It was a snazzy little thing with red interior and a red pinstripe along the side. These vehicles weren't that unusual in Beverly Hills, but what were the chances of seeing Lucille again when they'd just parted company?

At the next signal, she ran a red light, made a left, and veered across Robertson. It was her all right, but she was in a hurry to be somewhere. It was only when she made the turn that he realized she wasn't alone. She had company.

Sawyer.

Huh. Nah. Now I'm imagining things. Monty wouldn't risk a ticket trying to follow her. Besides, his ice cream was melting. He turned around again, heading south toward the family house on Wooster, two blocks east of Robertson. He parked in the driveway and sat for a moment, finishing the last bite of his cone. *So what if Sawyer and Lucille are hanging out? They're allowed. But he said he'd call.* Monty mentally rolled his eyes at himself. *I am so damned lonely. That's the problem.*

He licked his sticky fingers and got out of the car with his shopping bags. It felt weird to see the house minus the blue-painted roof on the porch, the blue door, and blue window trim and shutters. The Spanish-style house hadn't come with the blue. That had been his father's doing. Haint blue, he'd called it. Apparently, in the south, where Monty's parents had come from, haint blue was used to ward off ghosts because it was the color of water, and according to legend, ghosts couldn't cross it.

Monty had asked his father a few times, "Are we expecting ghosts, Dad?"

To which his father had grumbled, "You never know."

Now his mom had removed the blue, and inside, she'd gotten rid of a lot of Dad's religious stuff. It had creeped Monty out growing up, and he didn't miss the giant crucifixes, Jesus statues, or the strange glass balls he'd hung on trees in the backyard. Many of the glass balls were still out there, but each day, the place felt more and more empty.

"I'm home," he called out, his voice echoing as he walked inside. *How weird. I never heard myself echo before.*

More stuff was missing. Obviously, his mom had done more spring cleaning, removing her wedding photos from the hallway. Only one remained. It was her in her wedding dress from 1967. He knew the family story well, of course. That his parents had met in college in Atlanta, Georgia. Their families were pure southern. The day they married, it took place on a former plantation house on Edisto Island in South Carolina.

Hey, Sawyer's from South Carolina, but I bet his family's more normal. Probably more like Charleston than the islands.

There was something about the photo that always struck him as odd. He couldn't put his finger on it because his mom was a lovely bride. She made him think of a young Julie Walters. She hadn't aged well though and looked like Julie Walters' cranky Grammy these days. So, what bothered him about the photo? He studied it with a critical eye. Maybe it was the dress. She said she'd inherited it from her own mom, who'd married in the forties. She'd made some adjustments to it.

"You should have seen all the frills and beading," she'd said in the past. It had long sleeves, a throat-high neckline, and a gaudy, crown-shaped tiara.

What was I expecting? Even though it was 1967, would she have married in a mod-style mini-skirt?

His mom said the ghosts of former slaves had haunted the

wedding and caused them a lot of grief. A curse, she said but would never clarify. His parents had waited thirteen years to have him, and as a kid, it had been embarrassing to have the oldest parents in the class.

His father said curses didn't exist yet kept filling the house with religious icons. His fetish was so bizarre that Monty never invited his friends over. He'd relished being invited elsewhere. For most of Monty's childhood, his dad drove him and his mom on day trips to weird towns like Angels Camp in Northern California, hunting for religious relics. He bought a lot of stuff online after Monty and his mother filed credit card disputes with brick-and-mortar antique stores that sold the old man total rubbish they claimed were relics.

Most recently, he'd carted home a statue of Saint Jude from a yard sale.

It turned out to be stolen from a church in Mississippi. That had been a difficult one to explain to the police.

His father's troubles seemed to really escalate with the California lockdown. By the time the cheese shop was looted and damaged, he was in his bed praying all day to Saint Jude, the patron of lost causes. He'd also disappear in the middle of the night, usually in nothing but underpants. He'd hand out cash to total strangers, which wasn't bad. But the phone calls from kindly police officers saying they'd found him lying in gutters or sleeping on park benches were very much out of character.

Aricept had stopped working, and Monty Senior's doctors said his Alzheimer's symptoms were increasing. Then came some violent episodes that had become unbearable for Monty's mom. She was constantly calling Monty, and he'd come over to help. A couple of times, he took the brunt of his father's frustration when the old man would lash out for no real reason, then cry like a two-year-old.

"You have no idea what I've done for you!" he'd scream.

Monty's mom couldn't handle him anymore, and three

weeks ago, they'd found the perfect place for him. It had taken days to move him in. The first day, they let his dad come home again to spend the night, but his parents no longer slept in the same room. In fact, his dad had been sleeping in Monty's childhood bedroom for some time. Monty didn't care. As far as he was concerned, that bedroom didn't exist. But his dad seemed to be having lengthy conversations with imaginary friends late into the night. Finally, he accepted he had a new residence.

He was well looked after and had even made a few friends. In fact, he'd told Monty the day before that he had a new girl-friend.

"What about Mom?" Monty had been shocked.

"Who?" His father seemed bewildered.

Monty soon learned that old lives were quickly forgotten when Alzheimer's patients were displaced.

Monty's mom laughed at the mention of a girlfriend. "Well, that just dills my pickle. She's welcome to him. He's useless in the sack, anyway. Has been for a long time."

Monty moved in full-time when his dad moved out. He'd always been uncomfortable with the religious paraphernalia in the house and the blue glass balls his father had hung from every tree outside in the backyard. Still was, for that matter. The balls swung and clicked against each other, even in the smallest breeze. For some reason, the sound had always seemed ominous. Now with many of them gone, he didn't feel the heaviness, the relentless oppression of his father's pi-ous mania.

In the kitchen, Monty unpacked everything. He no longer had to open each food item and take a bite as he had to when his dad was there. Because of his severe mental issues, his dad would take new food items and return them to the store. More often than not, the wrong store. With bites out of things like cheese and ice cream, he couldn't return them and would fly off the handle, saying Monty was ripping him off.

I don't miss his gale-force rages. "You want the cherry or almond ice cream?" He smiled across the open serving window at his mom.

"Oh, the cherry. And give me a teaspoon, sweetie. I want it to last."

He took her the ice cream and spoon and then returned to the kitchen to pour a fresh cup of coffee for her. She parked herself on the sofa in front of the TV in the living room and powered up the remote.

She tuned into a DVR'd episode of *My Lottery Dream Home* and called out, "I love David Bromstad. That's one dishy host." She said this each time she watched an episode of the show. "Why can't you date someone like him? He'd make this place look like a dream home, I just know it." Her eyes twinkled.

He shook his head. *I'd like to meet a guy like David Bromstad, too. And not just for his decorating tips.*

On TV, Bromstad was laughing and hugging a young couple who'd won three million dollars on a five-dollar scratch-off. He was so cute with them. Then Monty thought about Sawyer and wondered if it was too soon to call him.

Will he think I'm desperate?

"You've been busier than a moth in a mitten today." His mom paused. "You had a date, didn't you?" She was stirring the ice cream in its carton, making soup out of it.

He would never understand why she did that.

"No. I had lunch with two people." *Wish it had been a date . . .*

"Huh? Really? So, there wasn't a man?"

"Well, there was a man. But he was . . . Well, I met him and this woman at the Louis Vuitton store."

"What was his name?" She seemed way too excited.

These days he was sick of disappointing her, so he changed the subject. "The woman's name, get this, was Lucille Ball."

"Yes, I saw her. She's pretty. And she was all over you. Is there something you're not telling me? You like girls now?"

He gaped at her. "What are you talking about?"

"Your Instagram posts. And hers. I clicked like. You didn't notice?"

He squinted at her across the open-plan kitchen and living room arrangement and brought the coffee to her, sitting beside her on the sofa. He checked through his cell phone. To his surprise, not one photo he'd taken contained images of Sawyer. Even one he knew for a fact Sawyer had been in. *Wow. That is weird.* There were photos of Lucille, though. He noticed for the first time some of the odd looks people gave her in the store.

It was the missing photos of Sawyer that disturbed him, though. Even in Lucille's posts where the two had posed together. He'd seen them taking selfies together.

Yet in each photo, Lucille was all alone.

What the hell was going on?

"Think he saw us?"

Sawyer took a deep breath. "He was following us. So, what do you think?" *We should never have come out here before dark. Maybe I've ruined everything.*

"If he did see us, he didn't stay with us very long."

He passed a hand across his forehead. "Sorry. I didn't mean to bark at you."

Lucille reached across the seat between them and squeezed his knee before shifting gears and parked. "It's okay. I understand."

He blew out a breath. "I know you do." He tried to relax. "Think it'll be okay?"

She glanced across at him. "He's smitten. You need to call him tonight. But wait until dark. You don't want him to see us spying on him."

He fretted. "I had no idea he'd stop for food. He's sharp though, I'll tell you."

"Yeah. He is. What the hell possessed you to say that about the moon?"

"I'm desperate. Desperate men are full of stupid ideas."

"We have a week. It'll be okay."

Sawyer wasn't so sure. He would have made a move on Monty weeks ago but had been immobilized by . . . unseen forces. He tried not to worry, but time wasn't on his side. "What made you say you're a cheese expert?"

They looked at each other and laughed. And laughed.

"I needed that." Lucille wiped her eyes with the back of her hand. A good laugh always brought tears to her eyes. "I do like cheese, you know."

"Your idea of gourmet is a pack of Kraft singles."

"Hey. I meant what I said about that cheese with the maggots. I loved it. Okay, maybe slices a little bit more."

"Any other cheese you like?"

"I like the one with the maggots."

He looked at her. "You're really stuck on that one."

"I can still taste it." She smacked her lips together.

Sawyer could never tell when she was serious or when she was pulling his leg. He hadn't seen her, *been* with her, for so long, the novelty left him giddy. He touched her cheek. "I've missed you."

"I know you have. And I missed you. Now leave the moon stuff alone. We already agreed. That's my department. You just concentrate on your part. Okay?"

"Okay." But the truth was, he was still concerned.

"I have a plan you're going to love for tomorrow morning. You'll see. I'll win him over." Lucille's eyes shone with mystery. And intent.

"What are you up to?"

"You'll see. And you're gonna love me."

He smiled. "I already do." Sawyer twisted around in his seat. They were on Wooster, several houses away across the street from the Pellman home. *So close and yet, millions of miles away from him. Life is cruel sometimes. No. Life is one nonstop act of cruelty.*

What if this fails?

"So. We sit and wait." Lucille handed him a bottle of water.

He unscrewed the cap and drank half the contents.

"Better?"

He nodded. His stomach was in knots. What if the old man came home? Together they could handle him, but he knew the family would probably want him home for Thanksgiving unless Sawyer could stop them in the meantime.

They have to invite me, not him, to Thanksgiving.

"Oh, no," Lucille suddenly said.

He came back to the present. "What's wrong?"

"There's a problem."

His chest constricted. "What kind of problem?"

"None of the photos I took with you are on Instagram. You don't show up in any of his photos either."

"I will." He glanced up at the sky. "Give it time. I'm getting stronger all the time."

She slapped her dashboard. "Good. That's the spirit. Positivity. Holy crap. Look!" Her pale face turned even more ashen as she pointed a shaky finger across the road. A man walked down the street in the direction of Monty's house.

"Doesn't mean anything," Sawyer said. "He could just be walking by."

"I don't like it," she whispered. "Something's wrong. Very wrong." She took a sharp breath. "Oh, no."

Out of nowhere, a dark figure pounced on the young man, like a demented raven dropping from the sky.

"Don't move." Lucille's voice came out in a deadly whisper. She grasped Sawyer's arm, her nails digging into his flesh.

"Lu. You're hurting me."

"Sorry." She released her hold, her eyes filling with tears. "He knows, Sawyer. How will we ever get in there?"

He shook his head. He couldn't tear his gaze away from the young man who now lay in a puddle of blood across the road. A young man who was supposed to be him.

It happened so fast. I will not die today. He raised the bottle to his lips and took another drink.

"Home?" Lucille asked. Her anguished tone echoed the one in his heart.

I'm sorry. He sent the thought to the young man whose spirit had risen from his dead body and stood, uncertain, and alone, no help, no sign.

Just nothing.

The restless spirit stayed by the body. Sometimes, victims of violent crime didn't even realize they were deceased yet. Sometimes, life clung to them like a heavy winter coat, and they resisted moving on. The earth was full of them.

Death wasn't like that for me. When Sawyer closed his eyes, he saw it all as though it had happened yesterday. But it hadn't. It all took place such a long time ago. But he'd been trapped, and an angry, vengeful man had killed him.

Or tried to . . .

The angry man had beaten Sawyer, who'd tried to fight back, but it had been three against one. One man had swung an axe at his head.

Next thing I knew, I was in this floaty place. I can't explain it. I didn't see or hear anything. It was a feeling of peace and weightlessness. I didn't hear choirs of angels or see my parents or my deceased pets, but everything around me was a soft pink. I knew if I kept going, I would die. I would pass peacefully. But the next thing that happened was an image took over—a picture of Monty sitting on my front porch, staring at the road, waiting for me to come home. I knew I couldn't leave him here. So, I came back. I couldn't wait to go home and be with him. But he waited. And I was put in hell. A hell I've only just gotten out of.

Can I ever tell him we've waited so many years to be together? That I've been trapped in the moon?

Sawyer cried then. Hot, hot tears. Not only for his near-death, but the unknown man still lying there across the road.

"It's not your fault." Lucille put an arm around him.

"I know." In death, life, half-life, which was what he was living now, Sawyer knew what he needed was Monty.

Monty and the knowledge, no, the belief in their love, was what had kept him here.

He's the one. My life. He's my choir of angels. "I have to help that poor man's spirit," he said, opening the car door.

"No. Don't." Lucille pulled him back, made him close the door. She drove away with the headlights turned off as the sound of sirens and the flood of police lights—blue lights so bright they hurt the eyes—pulled up outside Monty's family home.

Monty was in the kitchen, making fresh coffee, surprised when sirens and lights shattered the evening calm. He cast a glance at his mom, but she remained immersed in her TV program. He walked down the hallway and opened the front door as two uniformed officers ran up the garden path.

"Sir," one of them said, hand on his holster, "Did you see or hear anything unusual tonight?"

"No, I didn't. What's going on?"

"Oh. Hi. It's Monty, right?" the second officer asked.

Monty glanced at him. "Yes. I recognize you. I want to thank you again for helping my dad that day. Really. You were wonderfully kind."

The officer looked pleased. "No problem. How's he doing these days?"

"We put him in assisted living." Monty looked past the officers to the activity on the street. "What happened?" His gaze fell on a heap of clothing and what looked like blood on the sidewalk between his house and the neighbor's.

"Somebody called us and reported an assault. Most likely a mugging. Third one this week. Did you see or hear anything?" the first officer asked again.

"No. Nothing." Monty had just realized he wasn't wearing a face mask, but neither were the officers.

"We've managed to keep the other two out of the media—" The second officer's voice disappeared beneath the whir of choppers overhead.

Monty had no idea there'd been any muggings at all. "I didn't hear anything. I was watching TV with my mom. Are you saying there were two other attacks? In this neighborhood?"

"On this street." The second officer gestured. "Is your mom inside?"

"Sure. Yes. You want to talk to her?"

"If we could." The first officer breezed past him, followed by the second. Monty detected the faint scent of Juicy Fruit gum.

He led the way to the living room where his mom was laughing at David Bromstad. He was mixing a homemade lockdown face mask using kitchen ingredients and eating half the stuff before he could slap it on his cheeks.

"Oh, he's so funny!" His mom turned and seemed shocked when the officers entered the living room. "Son, you didn't tell me we had company." She fumbled for the remote. She was now working on the second pint of ice cream and probably would have offered the two officers a bowl each if they hadn't started peppering her with questions.

"Ma'am, did you see or hear anything unusual tonight?" the first officer hollered over the volume on the TV set.

She muted the sound, staring at him. The flashing lights from the police vehicles flickered across the mirrors and many glass windows of the room.

"No. I did not." She turned to Monty. "What's all this about?"

"Somebody was killed out front."

She whipped her head around to the officers then back to Monty again. "Oh, my God. Who was it?"

"I . . . I don't know. I was in the kitchen making coffee, and I went to go check on the noise."

"I know that. But who was killed?" His mom's facial expression was one of complete terror. "Was it a man?"

The two officers exchanged looks. "Yes, Ma'am," the first one said.

"Oh no." She leapt from her seat and rushed out of the house.

Monty and the officers chased behind her. Monty hadn't seen her move so fast in two decades.

"Ma'am!" hollered the first officer.

"Mom!" Monty yelled, but she ignored him. For the first time, he remembered she was wearing pajamas, otherwise known as her coronavirus uniform.

Outside the house, an ambulance crew and a bunch of other officers had crowded around a young man on the ground. He'd been stabbed multiple times. Monty had never seen such horror. His mouth fell open as he saw ugly, deep gashes in the man's face and neck.

His mom let out a sigh of relief. "Never seen him before in my life. Come on, Monty." She threaded her arm through his. "Time for me to exfoliate."

What? What the hell was she talking about?

"I have your number," the second officer told Monty. "Can we call you if we need to follow up with you?"

Monty had turned cold with shock. "Yes, of course. I'm sorry. My mom —"

"No problem." The second officer cut him off, then turned

to deal with the next-door neighbors standing next to him.

As Monty's mom dragged him away, he was certain a dark figure across the road was watching them.

Sawyer.

What the hell?

He blinked and looked again. No. Not Sawyer. Man, I'm seeing him everywhere today. It was a bunch of looky-loos. But he was certain he'd seen Sawyer. And he'd seen him earlier, too.

What's going on? Three dead men on this street? Is he some kind of psycho killer? Just my luck. I always did have a colossal lapse in judgment when it comes to men.

Inside the house, his mom closed and locked the front door. "I must have missed a haint," she whispered. She turned to peer out of the peephole.

Oh, brother. I swear she's going loopy too. "No, Mom. You got all the paint. No more blue. It's all white now—"

"I'm not talking about the paint. I'm talking about the haints. I thought I got them all. We need to check the garden."

"Are you talking about the glass balls in the trees?"

She skewered him with a penetrating gaze. "Yeah."

"There are some still out there. I—"

"I'll get the ladder. But not tonight. Too many cops. Mind you, they all seemed useless if you ask me. All hat and no cattle."

He bit his lip. She had no shortage of wacky Southern sayings but now was not the time to laugh.

"I should go out and see if I can help."

"You can't help them. But you can help me. We can't look now, though. They'll think I'm strange. They'll think we're strange. First thing tomorrow, though. Okay?"

She patted his chest with both hands so hard he reeled backward, then spun on her heel, striding into her bedroom. "Get an early night," she instructed. "The hunt begins at dawn."

He stood for several long moments, staring at her closed door. What the hell had gotten into her? She never went to bed this early. He checked his cell phone — six-forty p.m. It got so dark so early these days at this hour he often thought he should be in bed himself. He waited for some sound on the other side of the door. The only thing was her TV, a small portable unit he'd bought for her private use. She was watching *My Lottery Dream Home* again.

And he was as bewildered as ever.

In the living room, he turned off the TV. The police were still out front, and media crews were out in full force. He became aware of people with cameras surrounding the house and lowered the blinds. He closed the kitchen windows, too, thankful that his ex had his dog and that Riley wasn't here to run around barking at everything that moved.

Oh, I miss that dog. Monty thought of his ex-lover, Luke. *Don't miss him at all.* His dad had inexplicably hated him, which had caused continuous drama in Monty's relationship with Luke.

At that moment, he couldn't stop thinking about the murdered man and the ones who'd been killed before. Right here on this street. *Who? And why?*

Monty finished making a fresh cup of coffee, got out his laptop, and checked online news reports. Nothing. Maybe it was too soon for the Internet vultures, er, reporters to get the news out there yet. The officer had told him they'd managed to keep the earlier attacks out of the media, but how? It seemed now the media was here in force. He checked various news and crime sites and found reports of two attacks in the neighborhood over the past several days — no mention of homicide. He bookmarked them, surprised that more hadn't been made of these incidents.

Then came a live news report from outside his neighbor's house. The eager-looking reporter wore a paper mask near his chin and said, "This just in, Greg. Los Angeles Police Department officials said they are chasing new leads in the case of three men murdered for their wallets in the Crestview neighborhood. This normally calm and peaceful area has been very active since last week."

The reporter read from a piece of paper in his hand. "The first killing we know about was a young man named Jaime Torres. He was stabbed as he crossed the street near Pico. Right at the intersection. He'd just left the ATM, and police believe he had been followed by his assailant, and when he resisted giving him his wallet, he was stabbed and robbed. He died on his way to the hospital. Three nights ago, Russell Morse was stabbed as he went for a jog along Wooster. He was robbed as well. We are still awaiting the identity of tonight's latest victim. His wallet is missing, and the detectives on the scene still don't have any idea who he is."

The news coverage included flashes of Monty's house and his neighbors' property. The reporter's voice boomed over the visuals.

"None of the residents here know who the victim is. Nobody appears to have seen him before. Police say his death was overkill. That he was stabbed over forty times. A particularly brutal killing. Back to you in the studio, Greg."

Monty muted the rest of the coverage. *Forty times*. He sat back in his chair and wished he had seen the victim before. Or that he could offer some help.

Why do I get the feeling that all hell just broke loose?

CHAPTER THREE

Sawyer stood on the doorstep of The Cheese Guy shop and took a deep breath. He was certain he could smell cheese, but anyone peering through the huge glass door and big picture window could see there was none. Not a single piece. The store was devoid of all food products from what he could see. There was a smattering of culinary accoutrements. He focused on a rustic-looking shelf. His razor-sharp eyes took in the cheese cookbooks, cheese-shaped salt and pepper shakers, a couple of chefs' hats, and a pair of cheese wedge-shaped candles.

But where was the cheese?

Lucille hadn't explained what had happened, and touching the door handle, normally a big giveaway for Sawyer, didn't reveal a thing. He closed his eyes and concentrated. The door handle was new. *Why?* What had happened that so much of the store was new? He scrutinized the beautiful décor inside. Monty had done a wonderful job revamping it. He'd done away with the haint blue archway at the entrance, and Sawyer luxuriated in being able to stand on the straw welcome mat that read, *Cheese Please.*

He touched the wall beside him, and a frisson of some hidden, silent terror shot through him. He took an involuntary step back. Jumbled images skittered across his mind. *Danger.* He needed to move away and watch from across the road. Holding his burning left hand in his right, pain tore through him as though he'd lit a match to it.

I've only ever experienced such sheer and utter hatred once in my life. Damn! What the hell happened here? Sawyer frowned, trying to clear the riot of images that wouldn't let go of him. He took another deep breath.

Monty's coming. He's close. Sawyer moved fast. *The last thing I want is for Monty to think I'm stalking him. Okay. Maybe I am a little but only because I'll be out of time. And we'll never get our chance again.*

From his vantage point just inside the opening to a fancy medical office building directly opposite The Cheese Guy, Sawyer studied the store's outward appearance. It had a vintage look with a mix of French and British. Monty had painted everything a glossy butter yellow and milk white. Very inviting.

Sawyer liked this section of Brighton Way because he knew there was only one other eatery on the street. A breakfast bakery. If Monty could reopen with tantalizing cheese dishes and baked goods, he'd clean up.

Where the hell's Lucille? She's been so secretive this morning. Sawyer flicked his gaze away from the shop long enough to fire off yet another text to her.

Hello? Lu?

Nothing.

Not a word.

It wasn't like her. But Sawyer knew in his heart that she was okay, so he didn't worry.

She's my girl. And I love her. Whatever she's doing, it's for my sake as well as Monty's.

I hope.

Oh, man. Can she read my thoughts when we're not together?

Lately, the spiritual, mental, and emotional connection between him and Lucille was strong. Very strong. *Too bad we don't have a physical one. That would solve all my problems.* With a jolt, he realized his hand had stopped burning. *Good.* Another deep breath, and he almost missed Monty bounding up the two small steps to his front door. He seemed agitated as he unlocked it, glanced up and down the street before slipping inside and closed the door behind him again.

Super stressed. He's running late.

Sawyer waited. And watched, able to pick out Monty in the near-empty store. He turned on lights, some music—French café music, how apt—and then opened the door again. He seemed shocked when he spotted Sawyer across the road, watching him. Sawyer gave him a little finger wave and moved forward. *Man, his face is turning white. Is he ... is he afraid of me?*

"Good morning, Monty!"

Monty nodded, looking distracted. "Morning."

"Your shop looks amazing."

"Thanks." He looked up and down the street, his face as white as a sheet.

Sawyer glanced at him. "Anything wrong?"

"Have you been here long?"

"No," Sawyer lied. "Why?"

"Ah. I'm waiting for my cheese vendor. I've texted twice already this morning to confirm our ten-a.m. appointment. No response."

"Cheese, Louise." Sawyer rubbed his chin.

Monty chuckled. "That's a good one. Cheese, Louise." He rubbed his chin too. He blinked then stopped. "And you didn't see anyone else here?"

"No. Nobody. It's just ten now. Maybe he's just running late."

Lucille had told Sawyer she didn't think the cheese seller would show. She'd had quite the conversation with Monty the day before and had extracted a lot of information from him. She'd claimed she'd save the day. *She'd better be quick about it. I don't know how many more setbacks Monty can handle right now.*

"This reminds me of that Monty Python sketch. You know. The one with the cheese shop that has no cheese, but the owner insists it's the best cheese shop in town."

"I do recall it," Sawyer lied. *Who or what is a Monty Python?*

"I gave him a deposit." Monty leaned against the door-frame. "Stupid, right?"

"Where did you find him?" Sawyer wanted to scream, *Are you crazy?* but resisted the impulse. He cherry-picked his words. "Not crazy. Trusting, sure. Where did you find him?" he asked again.

"He walked in a couple of days ago." Monty's Adam's apple wobbled crazily in his throat. "Tommy de Anzo's got a store in Grand Central Market. I checked him out. He's got great Yelp reviews. He said he's been visiting local businesses in person because shopkeepers are still nervous going downtown and getting too close to other people." He blew out a breath. "I should have just gone down there myself."

"Maybe." Sawyer wished he could text Lucille with one word, *hurry*, but she had to know by now that Monty would be getting frantic.

Monty's eyes were doing funny things. "Maybe he's stuck in traffic. He'll be here."

Sawyer doubted it, but he wanted Monty to be comfortable, not panicked. "Maybe. Yeah."

Monty seemed fascinated by something on the ground. "I was just going to make a coffee. You want one?"

"Yeah. I'd love it, thanks." Sawyer followed him into the store, swallowing hard. Each step he took past the entrance made him feel like a weak, sea creature. Tears stung his eyes, but the blurriness stopped after a few seconds.

Something's wrong. There's still hatred here. Sawyer's heart pumped crazily. He started getting tunnel vision, and taking a few short steps made him dizzy.

"You okay?" Monty's voice came from somewhere far away.

I can make it. "Yeah. Fine." *Boy, I'm getting good at lying.*

From nowhere, snowflakes blew around him. Soothing. So soft. He came back to himself. He'd survived the remnants of the haint. He smiled at the song streaming from invisible speakers.

"Hey, you know this song." Monty smiled at him.

"Sure, I do. It's *L'aigle Noir*, Black Eagle. Probably the most famous song by Barbara."

"I discovered her last year." Monty moved behind the counter and fiddled with a coffee maker. "My dad bought this machine. Doesn't seem to like anyone but him. Let's see if I can get it to behave."

"Let me try." Sawyer tried not to hum along with the lyrics as he fiddled with the elaborate stainless-steel spaceship with the letter R emblazoned on the front. *What the hell is this? Why did I volunteer to look stupid?*

"Out of my way, stupid."

Sawyer let out a sigh of relief. "Lu."

"I love these machines." She put down the containers she was holding and ran her hand over it.

Monty pointed at the containers. "What have you got there?"

"I told you I'd bring samples. Two different things. A *flognarde*, which is a traditional French dessert made with a sublime custard. I also made a special apple, cranberry, and cheese stuffing since it's Thanksgiving coming up."

Monty scrunched up his nose. "I don't think —"

"It's made with *comté* cheese." Lucille seemed so proud of herself.

Monty's eyes widened. "How did you get hold of comté?"

"It's one of my faves."

Sawyer was stunned. She must have driven all over town and spent all night putting these two dishes together. And to top it off, she was wearing a vintage black Chanel twin set. *Where the hell did she find that? What a woman.*

She touched Sawyer's shoulder. As usual, she read his

mind. "You look handsome. Nice white shirt. I think you ironed it." She giggled. "And those pants. Wow. Tight in all the right places."

He stared. What had gotten into her?

She winked at him then lifted the lid on the flognarde.

"Oh, my." Monty's face swam with a mixture of emotions as he took in the large pie-looking creation dotted with fragrant, baked fruit. "It smells fantastic."

Sawyer, too, was impressed. "I smell plums." He almost salivated as the combination of fruit and custard floated up to him.

"Yes. Fresh plums, peaches, blackberries, brown sugar, custard. Eggs, of course, and my secret ingredient . . ." She grinned at them both. "*Neufchâtel.* French cream cheese."

"Wow. You said this is a sample? Can we try it?" Monty's eyes were like orbs.

"I brought samples in plastic containers. Where's Freddie?"

Freddie? Oh, man. What the eff is he doing here? Sawyer didn't like the way this was going at all. He glanced at Lucille, who made a point of avoiding his gaze.

"Freddie!" She bellowed like a stevedore, which wasn't too strange since she'd worked as a stevedore once. Though the less said about that phase of her life —

"Coming, missus." Freddie came in, holding four cardboard boxes. He looked like a thug. Which he was. Bald. Big. But cute. If you liked your men to have an extra side helping of menace.

"Oh, my." Monty's face went red. His eyes took on a glazed look that might have indicated total terror or awe. Or both.

Freddie grinned at him.

"Thank you, Freddie." Sawyer hoped his clipped tone conveyed the iciness he felt. He understood why Lucille had brought him, but he wanted the guy gone. He traded glances with Freddie, who knew what he wanted.

"Cheers," Freddie said, plonked the boxes on the counter, and walked out of the store.

"He's got a kind of Jason Statham thing going on, doesn't he?" Monty's voice came out in a strangled whisper. "Why do I hear piano music around him?" He seemed to sense the hooded looks exchanged between Sawyer and Lucille.

"What? What did I miss?"

"Nothing." Sawyer shook his head and heaved a sigh of relief.

Piano was Freddie's last name, and he came from a long line of piano tuners who doubled as, ah, hitmen. When a target heard music when Freddie was around, it meant they were under his protection.

When neither Sawyer nor Lucille said anything, Monty gestured toward the boxes Freddie left on the counter. "What's in these?"

Lucille grinned. "Your samples."

Monty's face lit up. "Can we try them?"

"Of course, we can." Lucille lifted the lid of one of the boxes.

Sawyer was astonished to see tiny plastic serving cups containing samples of the flognarde. They each grabbed one.

Monty downed his portion quickly, then reached for another cup. "Oh my God. This is better than sex."

Sawyer laughed. "Who have you been having sex with if this is better than that?"

"Just myself. You know. Paddling the pink canoe."

When Sawyer and Lucille both laughed, his face turned crimson. "Me and my big mouth. Guess I should have another sample." He shot Lucille a happy grin. "Just to be polite."

"Try the stuffing." She slid a knowing glance at Sawyer. "We can let our customers try it. I'm so glad LA has eased its restrictions, and we can let people sample again. We can give them instruction cards, and they can make the recipes themselves. With your cheese, of course."

Monty's face fell. "But I don't have any comté right now."

"Freddie!" Lucille let loose with an ear-piercing scream.

Freddie walked in carrying heavy containers, followed by three little Pianos, also carrying smaller coolers. Monty's mouth dropped in a surprised O.

"Aren't you all cute!" He grinned at the boys.

"I ain't cute," one of them said.

"I am. Can I try the cheese?" another one asked.

"No. It makes you fart," Freddie responded.

The kid looked devastated.

Monty laughed, and when Freddie's back was turned, Sawyer sneaked the three boys sample cups.

Lucille handed Freddie boxes as she removed the food items. He left with one load, and she turned her attention to Monty.

"I took the liberty of ordering all the different cheeses I could think of. Of course, by tomorrow, your vendor will show up." Lucille's voice fell to a low mutter. "If he knows what's good for him."

She commandeered the unpacking of more boxes and cuddled the little Pianos, who always reminded Sawyer of tiny piranha fish. He was petrified of the boys. They looked like their father, and each had his head shaved. The better for looking dangerous, Sawyer supposed. The only baby Piano that Sawyer could handle was a cute little tyke called Hamish. He was probably guarding the family's van. Hamish looked adorable but could lay on a savage beating with his fists that could put a grown man in the hospital.

For months.

Nobody had ever explained the spirit world to Sawyer, but he'd had a recent, fast education that left him tiptoeing around the, er, nebulous people around him.

"Hamish says hi." Freddie shot Sawyer a ferocious grin when he returned.

"Say hi back to him, please." Sawyer had no idea why Hamish liked him, but he was grateful for it.

"Thank you! All of you. I don't know what else to say." Monty's voice cracked as the Pianos walked out with their equipment again.

Lucille rushed around, placing cheeses of all descriptions in the glass cases.

"Oh. They left a box." Monty grabbed at the box on the counter. "It weighs a ton."

"That's a special surprise. Open it." Lucille gave him a warm smile. "Here. Like this." She held a long cord that had been wrapped around it and tugged.

The sides of the boxes fell away. Sawyer stood, awed by the magnificent creation made out of cheese.

"Oh!" Monty leaned forward. "Oh, my goodness. That's amazing. It's The Magic School Bus, isn't it?"

"It is indeed."

Sawyer joined in the gawping as they all took in the sculpture of a yellow bus complete with cheese wheels, children peering out of the carved windows, headlights, the whole nine yards.

"It's not edible, but we'll be able to put it in the window, and we can take orders for the edible kind. It's made of forty pounds of cheese. Thirteen different varieties. You'll be able to sell it for special events at about six hundred dollars a bus."

Monty stood, speechless.

"People will pay that, especially in Beverly Hills." Lucille couldn't stop smiling. "This has been waxed and spray painted in nontoxic lacquer so it can't be eaten but don't those wheels look yummy?"

"They do." Monty touched the bus in wonderment. "I swear I can smell cheese!"

"Yes. The smell will last a week, then we'll need to freshen it." Lucille glanced at Sawyer. "Help me get it to the window, will you?"

He scrambled to comply as Monty dipped into the box with the cheese stuffing samples. "Mmmm, oh, this is good." He looked stunned. "I didn't think I would want to try a cheese stuffing, but this is—" He blinked then frowned. His face flushed as though he were drunk. "Wait. When did we get a cheese bread mix? Or—a cheese and rosemary scone mix? I have a shop full of cheese. Where did it all come from?"

Lucille looked nervous for a moment, then a refined-looking woman in a pale pink vintage Chanel twin suit stepped into the store. She could have been fifty or eighty. Sawyer had no idea which. Closer inspection, however, showed that her face had been pulled so tight from what appeared to be many plastic surgeries, she could whisper in her own ear. She must have been lovely once.

Realtor. Sawyer pegged her as one immediately.

She walked in, an astonished look on her face as she took in the spectacle before her. "That's weird." She kept turning her head, finally reaching a finger beneath what Sawyer knew was a wig to scratch at her scalp. "I could have sworn I came by an hour ago, and the place was empty."

"We refrigerate the cheese at night." Lucille whipped a serving tray out of one of the boxes. "Would you care to try a sample of our new offerings? This is a flognarde, and over here, we have cheese, apple, and cranberry stuffing. It's to die for."

"No. No thanks." The realtor looked troubled. "I don't understand it. I came in to let you know I have a client who's had his eye on this place. I know you have a five-year lease. He was going to offer you fair market value . . ." Her flat gaze fell on the superb cheese bus. "That's . . . really something."

"Isn't it, though?" Monty looked ecstatic.

"Somebody told me you were going out of business. Especially after you got vandalized three weeks ago."

Monty seemed angry. "We've discussed this already, Donna. I have no interest in giving up my business. Why would I do that, just when I'm open and running again?"

Three weeks? The store was vandalized that recently? Sawyer's thoughts raced. That explained the new front door handle, the paint. Not to mention the wall of fury he encountered coming in here. Sawyer tried to tune into the destruction that had taken place. Who would do such a thing? He'd felt it when he walked in, and the effects still disturbed him.

The realtor handed Monty a business card with her photo on it. Sawyer glimpsed her name. Donna Harrigan. She walked around as though she owned the place. "I miss the blue paint you used to have."

"I don't." Monty sounded vehement. "Are you sure you wouldn't like to taste some cheese?"

She gave a sneer. "I find it hard to believe the flognarde could be anything near . . . authentic."

"Try it." Lucille held a silver tray toward her. "I promise that you won't regret it."

"We'll see about that." The old lady — for Sawyer was certain she was old, as well as being rude — looked into the sample cup as though it might bite. She hesitantly took the tiny plastic silver fork that Lucille handed her. "Cute." The old lady turned the implement over in her fingers then dug into her slice of heaven. Her whole expression changed. "Oh, that's delicious." She glanced at Monty. "It has a slight tang. What is that?"

"Cream cheese." Lucille handed the woman a second sample. "We have a recipe card for it, or you can always order one from us."

"Cream cheese, you say? But it's perfect." The old lady worked on her second helping. Suddenly, she glanced at the window again, shaking her head. A fine sprinkling of confectioner's sugar dusted her nose. "I still don't understand. This morning, this store was empty. Empty, I tell you! *Empty!*"

"An optical illusion." Lucille smiled like a tomahawk. "After the vandalism, on top of the one during the riots, well, we can't be too careful, can we?"

The old woman held her sample cup aloft. "An illusion, you say? You mean I could go out now and look in the window, and it will seem empty in here?"

Lu nodded. "That's what I said."

The old lady dashed out the door.

"You owe me big," Lucille rasped to Sawyer as the old lady stood at the windows, nose glued to the glass.

"I know it," he whispered back. Wait until he told her about what he went through walking in here.

The old lady came back inside again. "But what did you use? Double glaze? Is it a new kind of glass?"

"It's magic." Lucille bounced on her toes, no easy feat in her high heeled black boots.

The old lady shook her head and dumped her empty sample cups on the counter. "It's marvelous. That's what it is." She gave them an imperial, royal wave and left the shop.

Monty swiveled a glance from Lucille to Sawyer and moved outside the store, gazing through the windows. He returned, peering at Lucille, and said, "Tell me. Please. How did you do all this? Are you a witch?"

"No, darling. I'm a boo hag."

"A boo hag?" Monty was certain he'd misheard, or she was joking, but she seemed serious. When she didn't respond, his senses vibrated on red alert, but he couldn't pursue the question. Three people had just walked in, and he realized it violated the city's ordinance of having no more than five people in the store at one time.

That's okay. The law means five customers. Monty couldn't move, though. There were more people outside, peering in the windows. *Holy Toledo!*

Lucille sprang into action picking up two loaded sample trays. "Help me, will you?" she asked Sawyer and headed outside.

What the hell is a boo hag? Monty stood and watched. *Maybe a boo hag is a nicer way of describing a fag hag. Yes. That's it. Man, I hope so. I'm afraid to Google it.* He found his feet again and moved behind the counter, stunned at the volume of business that appeared out of nowhere. He hadn't even organized a float for the till yet, but most people handed him credit cards. Many places had gone cashless since the pandemic. He wasn't one of them. He'd plugged his card machines in the day before, and they were up and running.

Monty's heart sang as he dumped Harrigan's business card in the trash and wrapped endless pieces of cheese. He even sold the cheese salt and pepper shakers that had been sitting in the storage room for months and took a cheese bus order for a bridal shower.

Phew.

The store emptied, and another group walked inside. Monty wondered if somebody had paid the crowd to come here, but everyone who entered seemed to really want to be here. Almost everybody had bought something. He glanced out of the window and was astonished to see Freddie the delivery guy across the road, a music baton in hand, conducting some invisible orchestra. Monty blinked, and Freddie was gone.

I really need to stop imagining things. Monty smiled at the woman standing at the counter, examining the samples.

"Hi!" She beamed at him.

"Hi. Jan, isn't it?"

She marveled at him. "Good memory. I've only been in

here twice. Listen. Is Rima here?"

"No. She's not. Is there something I can help you with?" Monty tried not to bristle at the mention of Rima's name. She hadn't returned any of his most recent calls. In fact, he suspected she'd blocked him because he got the telltale one ring, and his calls shot straight through to voicemail each time he called. His texts seemed to go through, but he had not received confirmation that they had, which was unusual.

Laurent had sent a terse text back to his inquiries regarding a return to work.

Fuck no. Not in a million years.

Okay then. Monty tried not to worry. *I have help right now. Be in the moment.* He tried not to think of his father in the assisted living facility, then remembered he had Alzheimer's and would only be another source of concern. Especially when he got into one of his strange rages and accused customers of stealing.

"Can I help you?" he asked Jan again.

"Well, it's that recipe."

"What recipe?"

"The one for cheeseballs. You used to sell them here—"

"We still do." Lucille gently nudged him out of the way.

Monty stumbled over explanations for a cheese bread mix he knew nothing about with another customer. He tried in vain to focus but couldn't stop listening to Lucille's conversation with Jan.

Across the road, Freddie was doing pirouettes, which were astonishing for such a big guy. Baton still in hand, he seemed to be having fun.

I'm hallucinating. Holy cheddar. What's in the cheese stuffing samples?

"As I was saying," Lucille said, her tone soft and warm. "This cheeseball is made from the Pellman family's original recipe. I can give you a sample, and I'll also give you the recipe card if you'd like to make it yourself."

"No. Let me buy one. I can't bear to waste more ingredients." Jan's eyes widened as Lucille handed her a cracker loaded with a slice of cheeseball. She took a bite and closed her eyes. "That's it. That's the flavor I remember."

Lucille nodded. "It's an authentic southern recipe handed down—"

"She put bacon in hers!" Jan looked aghast.

"Bacon?" Lucille's mouth twisted in grief. "I'm certain that would have swamped all the other delicate flavors. Especially the fresh chives."

"This has fresh chives?"

"Yes, it does." Lucille gave her a dazzling smile.

"What about sour cream?"

"Sour cream?" Monty almost shouted the words. "Rima put sour cream in my cheeseballs?"

"And it tasted weird. Gave me indigestion for hours." Jan patted her stomach as though to help it get over the memory. "Let me take two of these cheeseballs. I can freeze one, right?"

"They freeze very well. Just wrap it in a lot of plastic wrap and a good freezer bag. It'll keep there for two months." Monty worked hard to let go of the rage he felt at Rima's sabotage. He'd worried about her stealing his recipes. If this was what she was doing to them, he'd have to get legal help.

He let Lucille complete the order and turned to apologize to the woman with the cheese bread mix.

She didn't seem fazed at all. "I want a cheeseball too. And two of the mixes. What's the scone recipe like?"

"Fantastic." Lucille laughed. "It's an unusual mix of sweet and savory."

"Sounds interesting. I'll take one." The woman smiled.

Monty suddenly realized he was running out of store bags. As if on cue, Sawyer materialized with a new batch. *Who needs Rima and Laurent when I have Sawyer and Lucille?*

Monty started enjoying himself. He had a lot of questions, but they would have to wait. In the meantime, he had a few

51

minutes to enjoy a cup of coffee from the contraption that Lucille seemed to have mastered without effort.

"This is good. How the hell did you do it?" he asked, making her laugh again. That seemed to be her standard response when she didn't want to answer something.

The day went by so fast his head was spinning, then it was time to close. Sawyer and Lucille helped him clean up, and he had no words for their kindness. But he had to try. Just as he attempted to formulate words of gratitude, he spotted Donna Harrigan, the realtor, watching the store from across the road. She'd been a perpetual nightmare since the beginning of the pandemic. He had no idea what her game was, but she'd been trying to intimidate him into giving up his store for months. And he wasn't the only one. Other shopkeepers had told him Harrigan, whom they all privately referred to as *Harridan*, had been putting pressure on them to give up their businesses.

"Don't let her get to you." Sawyer's strong, warm grip on his shoulder bolstered his courage.

"Thank you."

Sawyer nodded. "Freddie will deal with her."

What the hell does that mean? Monty freaked out for a moment, but across the road, Harridan and Freddie seemed to be having a pleasant conversation filled with laughter.

"Want to come to my place for a bit of R and R before heading home?" Sawyer asked.

"Yeah. Oh, yeah. Thanks."

Sawyer looked as happy as Monty felt.

"Okay you two. I'll see you in the morning. After I pay that vendor a visit at Grand Central Market." Lucille dabbed black lipstick to her lips.

"Lucille—" Monty began.

She held up a warning hand. "Don't thank me. Please. We've got a long way to go. Call your mother. I think she's left several messages for you and I will see you at nine o'clock. Biyee!"

"I—" How did she know his mom had called several times? The day had sped by, and he'd been so busy he hadn't checked his messages.

His mom had sent seven texts, which was normal for her. The last one said she was going to visit his dad. Good. That gave him a little more time.

He drove Sawyer up to his house and stopped out front.

"Pull up into the garage," Sawyer insisted and pressed a small black remote he took from his pocket.

Monty did as he was told, and for a moment, savored the quiet, velvety darkness inside the car once the garage door closed behind them.

Sawyer leaned in and kissed him. It was beautiful. Soft and gentle at first, it turned heated and frantic the next moment. By unspoken agreement, they got out of the car.

"Inside." Sawyer's tone was tense as he reached for Monty's hand and took him into the house.

Monty was aware of passing endless rooms until they came to one with a big four-poster bed in it. Sawyer pushed him down onto it and covered his body with his. Oh, man, he felt good. Sawyer's cock was hard as it ground against Monty's thigh. *Man, Lucille was right! Sawyer's black pants are tight in all the right places.* Monty tried unbuttoning Sawyer's shirt, but Sawyer growled low in his throat.

"No." He moved off Monty, and in a few swift movements, had all of Monty's clothes off. He shook his head, running his hands over Monty's body. "Better than I rem . . . imagined." He dipped his head, dropping kisses and licks on Monty's face and neck.

Monty writhed in desire, but it had been a long time for him, and fear crippled his yearning for more.

"Can we talk about Freddie?" He gasped as Sawyer licked

his forearm. The man was bathing him with his tongue. Nobody had ever done that to him in his life. For one sweet moment, he gave himself up to the sensation of tongue on flesh and swooned.

Oh, God. I could get used to this. "Freddie," he ground out at last. "There's something weird about him."

"Is there?" Sawyer moved down to Monty's fingers.

"You know there is." Monty couldn't believe he was ruining a romantic moment this way, but he had to know. "Is he, um, is he a boom hang like Lucille?" *There. I said it. Or asked it.*

Monty held his breath.

"Boo hag." Sawyer's gaze met his. "And no. He's not."

Right. As soon as I'm alone, I'm going to Google boo hags. I think I'm afraid to, though. "What is he then?"

Sawyer gave a slight grimace. "He's an ogre."

"An *ogre*?"

Sawyer shrugged. "A boogeyman."

"Holy shit! Like out of a fairytale?"

Sawyer winced again. "He's a more refined ogre than the ones you see in fairytales."

"Does he play piano?"

Sawyer seemed to pale and shifted on the bed beside him. "His last name is Piano."

"So, he doesn't play it? I heard music the whole time he was in the store. And ah, I think I saw him with a baton. And would you cut that out? Stop! Don't run your fingers or your damned mouth on my body. It makes me utterly stupid."

Sawyer laughed then. "Darling, he's a piano tuner."

"And an ogre." Monty's body went into orbit as Sawyer placed a kiss on his belly button.

Oh, my . . .

The pained expression returned to Sawyer's beautiful face. "On occasion, he's hired to protect people."

"And they hear music?"

Sawyer was silent so long, Monty worried.

"The ones who need his protection do. Yes."

"And I need protection?"

Sawyer's eyes blazed with fury for a moment. "More than anyone else I know. Now shut up and let me have some fun."

"I—" Monty couldn't complete his sentence. His brain had officially stopped working. He floated high above the ground, above the universe on a soft pink cloud. *What's happening to me? All I see is pink.*

The feeling of weightlessness held him in its gentle sway. Just as fast, the sensation subsided, leaving him feeling languid, and oh man, his cock was in Sawyer's mouth now.

Monty almost screamed at the intensity with which Sawyer worked on him. He felt like a girl, wanting to know when Sawyer had last had a man. The sheer joy of watching Sawyer pleasuring him brought some strange emotions with it . . . an almost actual religion to the experience. It felt as though his cock was being torn from his body, and yet it sent sensations of such acute desire shooting through him that he let out a shout when Sawyer released him.

Over and over again, Sawyer teased him to the edge of the cliff but would allow him to come. He murmured words Monty couldn't understand and didn't care to decipher. He wanted more. So much more. He languished in a haze of unspoken longing. He peaked, crested, but never came over the rise and then his heart stammered in his chest.

Sawyer chuckled. "You're ready."

He plunged his mouth back down Monty's shaft, and the orgasm Monty experienced was so intense, he screamed as he came.

And then his cell phone rang. He knew before he even looked that something was wrong. Very wrong. A text from his mom.

Your father escaped the nursing home. We've got to find him!

Ten seconds later came another text from her.

Kill the moon.

CHAPTER FOUR

Monty perched on the edge of the bed and re-read the text. One second the words *Kill the moon* were there. The next they weren't. *That's the story of my life these days. I keep seeing things.* He rose from the bed and swayed with a dizziness that frightened him at first. The last time he'd had an episode like this was when a strange, random fever hit him when he was eighteen.

The room began to spin out of control, and he clutched the edge of the bed for support. He went back. Back. Far and deep. He couldn't stop the vision playing out in his mind.

From somewhere distant, Sawyer kept begging, "Where are you? Stay with me."

Monty looked for him but couldn't see him. He'd gone back twelve years to the night he'd fought so hard to forget.

"I'm here. Oh, sweetheart. Don't you see me?"

"Hmm?" *What's happening to me?* Monty was back in his bedroom.

"Don't go there. Don't, sweetheart." Sawyer's voice coaxed him back to the present, but some invisible force propelled him back to the darkest time in his life. A time he never thought he would have to face again. He saw it all, like a movie, but fully emersed. In all its three-dimensional horror.

"Dad. Please don't lock me in here." He was lying on his bed, unable to move. At the time, he'd been delirious from fever. Now he saw his father handcuffing him to the bed. *Why? Why did he do that to me?* He remembered the fight and the strange malady that followed. *Eighteen years old, and they wouldn't let me progress from a single bed to a double. Oh, man. I can't believe it.*

His parents came and went.

I can't tell if it's day or night. Everything hurts. Why can't I stop remembering?

His mother came in. "Just confess," she'd whispered. "Then he'll stop hurting you." She cried as she said these words.

"But I didn't do anything wrong, Mom."

Monty had never come out to his parents, but somebody had seen him with another man looking *more than friendly* at the Horseshoe Coffee Shop in Sherman Oaks. According to his mother, his father was ashamed of him. According to his father, he might be better off dead.

"The fifth nail!" his dad kept screaming.

Monty had no idea what this meant at first until his mom explained that Jesus had been hammered to the cross with four nails made by gypsies.

"Legend has it there was a fifth nail that was never used because the gypsies hid the nail from the Romans. That fifth nail was supposed to be hammered into the Lord's heart."

"What's that got to do with me?" Monty's fever was so high, sweat ran in rivers down his face and along his neck. He could do nothing about it.

"I don't believe in it myself." His mother's hot breath aggravated his already burning flesh. "I just don't want your father to hurt you anymore. So, confess. Did you kiss another man?"

"No. I didn't. Why are you doing this to me?" Over and over, the questions ran through his mind. *Who made up this story? And why would they say anything to Dad? They know he's a religious nut. Man, I had such a great night that night. Too much coffee. Not enough food. I don't remember speaking to anyone in particular but got home a little after midnight.*

His father greeted him at the door, and without a word, punched him in the face. He dragged the sobbing, screaming Monty to his bedroom. That was the scary start of it—the worst of his father's unpredictable anger.

Monty's mother realized nothing had happened at the coffee shop. She'd asked Monty repeatedly, and after a few days, removed the handcuffs. Still, Monty couldn't move. He kept his gaze on the wall where he'd tacked a poster for *Felon*, a brand-new movie with the hot actor Stephen Dorff in the lead role.

Then his dad awakened him one morning, forcing him to drink a strange liquid that burned his throat.

He said it was to help me and made sick jokes about feeling the burn.

When Monty mentioned it to his mom, she said it was impossible that his father could have been in his room. "I'm the only one now with the key to the door."

But still, he didn't get better.

"What's wrong with me?" he'd ask her.

"It's an old family thing. You'll grow out of it," came her mystifying explanation, but she never elaborated on the illness.

Each time he asked, she brushed it aside, and he'd turn his head to gaze at the *Felon* poster.

I stayed alive to meet Stephen Dorff. I don't think I've even thought about him once since I recovered. His parents had kept him in the dark, literally, and figuratively for weeks. He was convinced he'd died at one point. Death seemed so much better than the terrible pain that swamped his body. Nothing worked. They wouldn't call a doctor, and his mother cried all the time.

One night he heard her screaming, "This is all your fault!" at his father.

His father blocked all medical care, and Monty, bedridden and immobile, couldn't even speak. When he finally croaked out the words, *Help me*, his mom sent for his Grammy.

Why am I remembering this now? Something bizarre came over Monty, and he fell back on Sawyer's bed, his whole body shaking with the effort to sit up and keep his feet on the floor. His gaze fell on Sawyer's lovely face.

I believe in love again. Monty shook his head, trying to loosen the thought.

"Are you okay?" Sawyer fretted over him. "Breathe for me. Please. Just breathe."

A cool compress was laid over Monty's burning forehead and eyes. Emotion flooded his senses as he recalled a weird dream that kept repeating in those weeks. A blue-black dream where he saw himself in a barn somewhere in his distant memory. Monty breathed heavily, not seeing Sawyer's room anymore.

"Tucker. Are you okay?"

Tucker? Who is Tucker?

Sawyer was beside him now, his arm around Monty.

"I'm fine. Honest. Just out of breath." Monty's voice sounded far away and tiny to his own ears. Snatches of memories, like little movies, skittered through his mind. His father's mouth twisted in utter hatred. The image frightened him, but he was starting to return to the present.

"Monty. Breathe."

He did, leaning into Sawyer as he remembered his Grammy coming to the house. She was furious with Monty's father. His mom hadn't believed his father was secretly attacking him late at night until scratches showed up on his dad's face and arms.

She'd called Grammy then.

When Grammy first arrived, he detected the persistent scent of juniper berries on her skin and clothes.

"Oh, my boy. She should have called me sooner." She ran

her hands over his face and body. The next morning, she brought in a *traiteur*.

In my state of delirium, I heard traitor. I already had one. My dad. Did I need another one? Then Grammy explained it for me. A traiteur, or treater in English, was a Creole medicine man or woman. I still have no idea where she found this lady, but Bathilde was amazing. I can still see her standing before me. All six feet eight inches of her.

Monty had found not just a savior but a protector in Bathilde. She was scary looking in her long white pants and tunic top with black biker boots, not to mention her frightening prognoses.

Her first day there, she told Grammy, "He has several ailments. He has a fungal infection. I'm thinking maybe meningitis. What has he been drinking? How much weight has he lost? When did he last eat?"

She awakened Monty several times with different types of hot tea and explained how each one was for *tansyon*, Creole for tension. She would fine-tune the herbs she used several times a day after tweaking his fingers and toes, muttering to herself, checking the palms of his hands, then peering into his eyes. She even lifted his eyelids to peer underneath them. A new kind of torture.

He liked her smell, though, which reminded him of good, clean earth and some kind of subtle flower.

"Camelia," she told him one morning.

It shocked him because he realized she could read his mind.

She woke him early one day. "Here. Drink this."

He struggled to rouse himself from sleep and sit up in bed. "What is it?"

"Did I ask you to question me, or did I ask you to drink the tea?" She glowered at him.

He was used to her ways by this time and knew she was fighting pure evil in the house.

She patted his head. "This be swamp lily, boy. It be bitter, but not burning. You haven't taken anything your father be bringing you, yea?"

"Yea, I mean, no." The teacup rattled in the saucer as he attempted to drink it.

"You'll get strong." Bathilde sat on the edge of his bed, staring into his eyes. She was so big she almost capsized his bed, but he held on tight. "He won't come in here anymore." Her voice dropped. "I just have to find that moon."

Her words mystified him. "What moon?"

"You'll find out. No more questions. Drink. I'd help you but some things you best be doing yourself. You need to let the dark side know you be a fighter."

"I *am* a fighter." He sipped at the steamy liquid, and it was bitter, like she said, but not nasty. It had a slightly medicinal, woodsy flavor to it. *Swamp lily*. He'd never heard of such a thing.

He slept right afterward, and she must have thought he couldn't hear her, but Bathilde's voice was as big as her person. He listened as she discussed his strange sickness with his grandmother.

"I'm going to recommend more of the swamp lily alternated every hour with warm rum, laced heavily with bee honey. The best you can find. If you can get some with the honeycomb in it, make sure he eats it. I'm thinking he has stomach parasites."

"How did he get those?" Grammy sounded distressed.

"I think the father be giving him things we know nothing about. Have you called the police yet?"

Grammy sighed. "No. My daughter refuses. He's out of the house, though. Staying with his brother."

"He's still coming in here, though. I caught him last night. He be crazy if he be thinking I'll deliver this boy to the devil."

Monty had an urge to sneeze but fought it with all his

strength. He wanted to know what was going on and Bathilde's conversation with Grammy was fascinating.

"Did your father give you meat? Did he give you any greens to eat?" Bathilde asked him when she woke him up later to drink more tea.

Monty couldn't answer either question but soon found himself propped up, being spoon-fed soup by Grammy.

She gave him baths filled with salts and herbs every couple of hours. He'd cry in pain. Walking to the bathroom almost crippled him. Back in bed, the stomach cramps kept him awake, writhing in agony all night. Blood came out of his ears, eyes, and mouth. And other parts, too.

And the traiteur came several times a day. Her look of concern not easing until Grammy told her she was certain Monty's father had given him contaminated water.

Grammy took over all of Monty's dietary needs. She supervised everything he ate and drank. "Don't touch anything your father tries to give you," she would say to him each day.

Monty gasped. *I remember now! He brought me a blue glass with water in it and slapped me in the face when I wouldn't drink it!*

"Don't," Sawyer murmured against his temple, giving him a swift, soft kiss there. "Don't think of it now."

But Monty couldn't stop the feverish tide of memories he'd held so deep.

Sawyer's sad words touched Monty's very core. "I could kill him for poisoning you. You have no idea."

What? What did he say? As Sawyer rocked him in his arms, Monty felt comforted, grounded. *How does he know? How could Sawyer have any idea what I'm thinking of?* The agony of those horrendous months came back to him. His illness had wrecked his relationship with his father, who had seemed angry that Monty recuperated. It had been his grandmother and Bathilde who had brought him back to life with their endless concoctions. His favorite had been Grammy's famous lemon-rice soup.

Well, it was more than that. When Bathilde had to go to the side of another young man under attack, Grammy had continued to protect Monty from his father's efforts to poison him.

Tears pricked at Monty's eyes. He still had no idea why his father had chosen to assault him with a near-fatal cocktail of thorium, lithium, mercury, barium, tin, and other metals, which introduced such high toxicity to Monty's system he barely survived.

How does Sawyer know?

He almost didn't care how he knew. Monty felt loved. It had been a long time since he'd experienced anything close to this sensation. *Holy heck. How can I even think of the L word? Maybe he's psychic. I don't know . . .*

His grandmother showed him pure love. His mom tried in a distant way, the only way she knew how. But his father. *Ugh.* His relationship with his dad had never been easy. During the height of Monty's illness, his father had kept placing some weird tinkly baubles in his bedroom window. He'd also tucked garlic into every available crevice and hung crucifixes everywhere. He had rarely come into Monty's bedroom once Grammy and Bathilde banished him. Once Grammy had been left alone to care for Monty, their epic fights had brought the police to the front door courtesy of the neighbors.

Monty had been devastated when his father returned to the house once Bathilde was gone.

One night, Monty had discovered fresh wooden slats nailed across his window. He'd freaked out, so his mom and Grammy took out the *scariest* objects — the crucifixes, the garlic, the religious texts plastered on everything. They'd uncovered his bedroom mirror, which his father had covered in blue fabric, but were afraid to remove the pieces of wood nailed over the window.

"He'll go mad," his mom had said. "We have to humor him a little." She'd removed most of the glass balls from his room and hung them in the trees in the backyard. Despite her recent strenuous cleaning, some were still there. In fact, there were tons of glass balls out there. Strangers thought they were attractive year-round decorations.

Monty found them creepy because they reminded him of that terrible time. He sucked in a deep breath when he found himself in a sweaty state, lying on Sawyer's bed.

I hope I'm not sick again. Monty groped for his clothing.

"Take a quick shower. It will help." Sawyer handed him a fluffy white towel.

Monty didn't resist. Water would help clear away the horrible visions in his mind. In the huge, elegant bathroom with the massive showerhead, he set the water pressure to rainfall and took a quick, energizing shower using soap from an unmarked bottle in the stall. He froze as soon as he smelled it in his palm. He would have known that scent anywhere.

Swamp lily.

He washed and dried in record time, then re-dressed as he called his mom. His thoughts tumbled when she didn't pick up. Frustrated, he sent her a text.

On my way.

"Are you okay?" Sawyer asked again, standing beside him in the bedroom. He held a glass of water toward Monty. But too many memories of his father's near-fatal cocktails made him balk.

He shook his head. "I gotta go. It's my dad."

"Don't go to him." A ripple of concern crossed Sawyer's lovely features. "Please, take a few sips. It's just water. Chilled alkaline water."

Monty took it. "Thanks." He drank, and the water soothed him. He relaxed a little.

He'd left the family house when he got better. Went away

to college back East. He'd kept his location private, even from his mom. He reflected on his life in hiding. *It would be so much harder to live off the grid nowadays with the Internet being what it is.* His life away from his parents had been peaceful. His mom had insisted that she didn't need to know where he was, but he needed to stay in touch. So, he had. He'd even returned to Los Angeles, and in the last couple of years, had forged a new relationship with his dad.

He'd come to work in the family's cheese shop, and his dad had taught him everything he knew. Things had been so friendly between them, Monty even began to think the horror that happened twelve years ago was all a nightmare. That his father wouldn't do that to him.

Ever.

In his heart of hearts, Monty had known it had happened. Survivors of trauma learned to live with the terrible things they'd endured. He'd learned to cope with an emotional limp.

Monty kept his private life so secret that his dad no longer thought he was gay. Monty didn't pretend to date women. He just never told his parents when there was a new man in his life—not that there had been many. Luke had been an exception, but by the time he came into Monty's world, Monty's mom had accepted his sexuality. His father was rapidly slipping into forgetfulness coupled with inexplicable bouts of fury.

His dad needed Monty in the store. And Monty still yearned for what he could never have—his father's love. And his approval. It didn't matter what Monty did. He would never have either of these things, and he'd learned to accept it, but it hurt. No matter how hard he worked, no matter how much time or love he gave his parents, he felt their acceptance of him was like one of their southern ghosts trying to cross the haint.

It would never happen.

And yet, he had an excellent buffer. Grammy. She had

moved in for good a couple of years ago, once Monty had returned to LA. Lovely Grammy. She was in Louisiana right now caring for her previously estranged sister, but she'd be back for Thanksgiving. She'd promised.

Sawyer touched Monty's cheek. "Can I take you somewhere?"

Once again, Monty jolted back to the present. "Ah. No, thanks. I have to . . . Oh, I just realized. My car's back in the parking lot. Do you mind taking me to my dad's—"

"Monty. Your car is right here in my garage. Are you sure you're all right?"

"Yes. No." He gulped. "Who's Tucker?"

Sawyer put a gentle hand on Monty's shoulder. "Please. Let me drive. You need to calm down. What's going on?"

"You can't drive my car," Monty snapped. "You're not insured for it."

"No. But I can drive *my* car."

"You have a car?"

"How do you think I get around?"

"I . . . I don't know. I thought maybe you could fly."

"With what? A broomstick?"

Monty laughed.

Sawyer's smile was so serene and reassuring it was hard to say no. Monty allowed Sawyer to escort him back to the garage, where a sleek black Datsun Z sat beside Monty's car.

"How come I didn't notice this before?" Monty touched the hood. As he climbed inside, he felt a familiarity with the vehicle he couldn't explain. "Is this . . . is this like an original?"

"Yes, it is."

Sawyer gave him another dazzling smile. "We had other things on our minds."

Monty's cheeks flamed at the mere thought of the way they'd rolled around on the bed together. He wanted more. So much more. "It's a 280Z Fair Lady. 1975." He paused.

"Right?" *How do I know this?* The next thought that came to his head was even crazier.

I know this car because it used to be mine.

He's remembering. Sawyer wasn't sure how he felt about it. Was it too soon? Would it make Monty go inward into some sort of fugue state? *We've waited so long. I must be careful now. Where the hell is Lucille? She should be here.*

The backdoor to the car opened, making Sawyer and Monty jump.

"Hey there!" Lucille climbed into the backseat, wreathed in smiles, and an electric blue dress.

"Snazzy outfit." Monty smiled, turning to her. He faced forward again and bent his head, pecking away at his cell phone. It pinged with an odd tone Sawyer couldn't identify.

Lucille tapped him on the shoulder. He caught her gaze in the rearview mirror. She lifted her shoulders in a slight *what gives?* gesture, but he shook his head at her.

"What's going on?" Monty's sharp tone cut into the silent dialogue going on between Sawyer and Lucille. Before Sawyer could think up anything, Monty continued. "They found my father on the roof of the assisted living facility. He won't come down until I go talk to him."

Sawyer and Lucille traded glances in the rearview mirror. He knew where the old man was but said, "Okay, we'll take you there. Where is it?"

"North Harper near Santa Monica Boulevard. There are two buildings. He's on top of the one closest to the Harper side." Monty checked his cell phone as he spoke. He seemed worried. How much was from what he'd remembered, and how much was his concern for his father's current circumstances?

Sawyer wasn't sure. He didn't care if the old man jumped. In fact, he wished he could give him a swift shove into the abyss. Not that he could or would say this. He marveled at what a good man Monty was. A very good man.

They rode in tense silence as Sawyer followed the onboard navigator's directions. He didn't need them. He knew exactly where the old bastard was staying. Not that he would tell Monty this unless it became necessary.

Traffic was light for nighttime in Los Angeles. The city was still not back to itself a hundred percent, but holidays always spelled travel for many people. With the pandemic, this meant road trips since people were afraid to fly. Sawyer had also heard train travel had become the big way to, er, get away.

But Monty's here. He's here with me, and I'll do anything to protect him. They arrived at the assisted care facility, and Sawyer had to maneuver around the ambulance and three police cars surrounding the scene. Sawyer paused with his foot on the brake as a uniformed officer approached his vehicle.

"Sir." Monty jumped out of the car. "My mom called me. My dad's on the roof."

"Not anymore. He came down again, but he's disappeared." The officer gestured to Monty. "You'd better go with Sergeant Anderson. We're having a hell of a time catching your dad."

Monty gave Sawyer a helpless look and went off with the cop.

Lucille tapped Sawyer's shoulder. "Go with him but stay out of the way. The old man can't see you."

"I know that." Sawyer couldn't help his irritation. "Sorry, Lu. It's just Monty. I'm worried about him."

Lucille got out of the backseat and whispered, "Hurry," in his ear as he got out of the car. She kissed his cheek, then jumped into the driver's seat and took off.

Sawyer drew a breath, scanning the scene for Monty. He sensed the old man's presence close by but wasn't afraid. *He can't hurt me, but he can hurt Monty.*

Monty was across the road walking with an odd gait, then suddenly stopped. He disappeared into a shroud of gloom, and Sawyer followed, keeping close to the shadows.

"You've seen him, haven't you?" a low, raspy voice sounded in the darkness.

"I—" Sawyer turned in the direction of the voice, but the old man wasn't speaking to him. He was addressing Monty, who stood in the middle of an alleyway piled with overflowing trash.

"Seen who, Dad?" Monty sounded exhausted.

Sawyer inched closer.

"You know who I mean. *Him*. The devil." The old man's voice exploded in a cackle and cough combined.

"No. I haven't seen the devil today." Monty kept his voice calm.

"Don't lie to me, boy! I know you better than I know myself." His voice carried despite the racket going on around them. "I know the devil. And so do *you*!"

"Oh, God, Dad. I hate when you get this way."

Sawyer inched around the corner of the building. As he listened to the exchange, he was stunned to see two officers approaching the old man from behind. It all happened so fast neither Monty nor Sawyer moved. The officers threw a large leather belt around him, and the old man screamed. He was strong. Punching, kicking, spitting, and biting, he fought the restraint, but the officers dragged him out of the alley and back toward the care facility. Sawyer jumped back against the wall, but the old man glimpsed him, his face contorting with rage.

"I knew it. I knew it! I knew you'd come back!" He screamed, resisting all efforts to get him back to the building.

Monty followed, exchanging looks with Sawyer. Even in the pale-yellow glow of the low-wattage streetlights, Sawyer knew the look on Monty's face.

Guilt.

He feels guilty for putting his father in this place when his father tried to do much worse to him. Lord, I love this man.

Sawyer stepped forward and put his arms around Monty, who held him back until his cell phone rang.

Monty checked the screen and sighed. "It's my mom. She's heading home. I should go with her, I suppose." He sighed again. "Except my car's in your garage. I should get it."

"I'll take you there." Sawyer mentally summoned Lucille to his side, and his trusty vehicle pulled up beside them seconds later. Across the road, Monty's father was being strapped to a gurney.

Monty turned, looking shaky but relieved as paramedics wheeled his father into the building. "He's really gone 'round the twist," he murmured. He turned back again, giving Lucille a tremulous smile.

Lucille hugged him, then got into the backseat of the car. Sawyer said nothing as Monty climbed into the front passenger seat. Sawyer slid in the driver seat and was about to put the car into gear when Monty started screaming.

Sawyer winced as he caught a glimpse of Lucille in the rearview mirror. She couldn't hide her real self from it. No boo hag could.

"What the fuck!" Monty screamed.

Across the road, a few remaining officers turned to glance in their direction. Sawyer drove off, restraining Monty from jumping out again.

"She's a monster!" Monty screamed. "A fucking monster!"

CHAPTER FIVE

Monty shook off Sawyer's hold, jumped out of the car, and ran. Cars skidded around him as he took off into the darkness, narrowly avoiding becoming roadkill.

He had no idea where he was going, but he'd never seen anything like the spectacle he'd glimpsed in the damned car mirror. *What the hell kind of creature is she?* In the next second, he mentally slapped himself. Had he really seen a blood-dripping monster in the mirror? The clatter of feet followed him, a chorus of voices calling his name. Screams died on his lips when hot breath slicked the nape of his neck. He didn't care where he went. He wasn't going back.

Monty hid in a clump of bushes outside somebody's stately home and waited as the footsteps faded away. He pressed uncomfortably against thorny branches and thought about the fifth nail.

His father's relentless paranoia had rubbed off on him. Now that he caught his breath, he realized he'd freaked out. But then, who wouldn't?

Wait. They were nice to me. If they meant to hurt me, they would have by now. Monty closed his eyes, remembering how hard his new friends had worked at the cheese shop. Lucille had said she was a boo hag. *What's a boo hag? I still don't know.* He stepped out of the bushes, checked up and down the street, but he was alone. Once he got his bearings, he tried to think about what he should do next.

Two doors down stood an apartment building with a well-lit vestibule. Somebody was moving furniture inside. Monty

71

slipped behind two men struggling up the wide stone steps with a hideous, leopard-print easy chair. As they grumbled and groaned under the weight of it, Monty couldn't help thinking of the character Ross, from the TV series *Friends*, directing his pals as they tried to get a massive sofa up the stairs, shrieking, "Pivot! Pivot!"

The thought made him smile. He still watched the show's reruns almost every night at eleven pm. He watched it because it made him happy. But now was not the time for levity.

He hunched beside a massive potted palm against the far wall of the lobby and Googled Boo hags. There was plenty to read, and he had a hard time wrapping his mind around snippets from different articles that clung like spiderwebs to his brain.

The Boo Hag of the Gullah culture is like the European vampire since it preys on the life force of human victims . . . Skinless, bright red in color, the boo hag has bulging blue veins and glowing eyes.

Monty freaked out for a moment and braced himself for the images in the articles he read. Yep. That was how Lucille had looked.

These monsters hide from sight during the day, or worse, walk around in the skin of a previous victim . . . To survive in the world of the living, they'll steal a living person's skin and wear it like clothes so that they can move amongst the living without suspicion. At night, they shed the skin and go looking for another victim to ride.

Jeez, Louise.

Another blog posted, *warning signs to let you know that a boo hag is close. First, the air will become very hot and damp. Second, the air will smell like something is rotting.*

Huh. He hadn't noticed either of those things with Lucille.

Like other evil spirits in Gullah culture, boo hags are repelled by indigo blue. If you paint the tops of your window frames indigo blue, boo hags won't be able to get through those windows.

He froze as he read on.

Originally, haint blue was thought by the Gullah to ward haints, or ghosts, away from the home. The tactic was intended either to mimic the appearance of the sky, tricking the ghost into passing through, or to mimic the appearance of water, which ghosts traditionally could not cross. The Gullah would paint not only the porch, but also doors, window frames, and shutters. Blue glass bottles were also hung in trees to trap haints and boo hags.

Monty re-read those words. His mom had removed every speck of blue paint around the house, but for years his father had kept the paint crisp with extra thick coats. And ever since Monty's strange sickness, had kept putting glass balls and bottles everywhere. His mom had removed most of them since his father had left the house. Come to think of it, mysteriously, when the store was vandalized, she'd suggested Monty *freshen* it by painting over the blue.

"It's oppressive, don't you think?" she'd asked.

He read on.

Salt, too, is a good boo hag repellent. A salted hag can't get back into its skin. But it's difficult to salt a hag since we can't pour it on people we deem suspicious.

How weird. Lucille had cooked with salt and seemed to have no trouble with it.

The easiest way to avoid a visit from a boo hag is to keep a straw broom or a brush with many bristles close by.

Monty re-read that line. *Huh.* Lucille had not only been unafraid of the broom in the store, but she'd also frequently swept the place during the work shift. As had Sawyer.

His stomach muscles clenched.

Sawyer.

What the hell do I do about him? And what the hell is he? Why did his image disappear from my Instagram photos? He clicked onto his Instagram page. And there he was. His image seemed a little faded, but he was there. *Wonderful, beautiful Sawyer. I had to be imagining things when I didn't see his face in the photos before.*

And wait. What about her? I like Lucille. But I know what I saw in that rearview mirror.

"You have to trust me," a gentle female voice said.

Monty glanced up to find Lucille, looking normal and human again. He was exhausted and more than a little frightened.

"Are you really like this?" he held up his cell phone.

"We're misunderstood," she said.

"I have no idea what's going on." He slumped to the floor and almost said, *Kill me now*. Whatever she wanted to do to him, he wished she'd get it over with. *What the hell am I thinking? None of this is . . . normal!*

"Not all of us are bad." Her voice a mere whisper. "Honest."

"So, you're a good bad spirit."

"I'm a good spirit. Like I said. My actions are sometimes misinterpreted. I can be bad when I want to be."

"And Sawyer?" Monty had just realized how much he wanted Sawyer to be real. And not bad. And not scary. And not—

"He's trapped."

"Trapped? Where?"

"No. No. He's here. But he's trapped."

He squinted at her. "By what?"

She paused. "Circumstances." Her eyes moistened. This was clearly emotional for her. Did big old boo hags cry? "You'll remember. You have to." Her troubled gaze met his, and she peered into his eyes for a long moment. "You really haven't figured it out yet, have you?"

What was she talking about? Whatever *it* was, no, he had no clue.

"I told you who I was. I haven't kept it a secret." Her worried look only increased as she extended her hand to him. It felt cool but real. Solid. Human. Not dripping blood or bulging with blue veins. She helped him to his feet. "Come on.

Let's get you home."

She was right. She'd said she was a boo hag, and he hadn't researched it. Would he have believed her if he'd seen the online articles first? Probably not. He'd seen her true state and still didn't believe it.

Outside, Sawyer stood against his car, looking pale and anxious in the moonlight. He also looked sexy as hell and covered the distance between them in three short strides. He took Monty into his arms, whispered, "It's okay. We'll be okay." He held Monty tighter.

Monty was torn between wanting closer contact, preferably naked, and running away again.

"We'll take you home." Sawyer took him by the hand and led Monty into the car's passenger seat.

A flash of memory struck him. "I—" A pull so strong it almost felt like a punch to the gut dragged him back to a warm night on a deserted road. A song on the radio—he could hear it as though the song was playing here and now.

Salad days are here again!

Monty gasped. For the second time in two days, those words shot into his brain. He could see himself clearly sitting beside Sawyer. They had stopped and began to kiss in the soft, dark air.

"I—" he said again.

Then a voice yelled, "Tucker!"

Monty gulped. There was that name again. Tucker! The memory, the feeling of that night vanished, and Monty plunged into a mental darkness he'd never experienced before.

"It's okay." Sawyer was beside him in the car, kissing his cheek, caressing his face and neck. "It's okay."

"Oh, my God. It was this car. This very same car!" Monty fought hot tears as he felt his soul being torn in two. "Oh, Sawyer, what the hell did I do to you?"

For a few seconds, Sawyer let the words fall over them. He knew exactly what had happened, but he didn't blame Tucker. Er, Monty. Neither of them was to blame.

"It wasn't you, baby. Never you. You could never hurt me." Sawyer took Monty's face in his hands and kissed him gently.

Poor Monty was shaking. It got worse the more Sawyer tried to comfort him.

Monty pulled away, putting a hand on the dashboard as though to steady himself. "I don't understand any of this. How do I know this car? How do I know you?"

Lucille was in the backseat now and reached over to Monty. She put her hand on his shoulder. Sawyer knew her touch would help. He hated seeing Monty in such distress. When he finally knew the truth, it would take everything in them to cope.

Did I do the right thing? Should I have left him alone? The thoughts rolled around in Sawyer's mind like giant tumbleweeds.

"Let's get you home," Lucille said. "We'll pick you up in the morning. I need to get in the kitchen and practice my vegan cheese recipes for tomorrow."

She nodded to Sawyer, who reluctantly started the car. He didn't want to go anywhere until he knew Monty was okay.

"Vegan cheese?" Monty's voice sounded distant and hollow.

"Yes! I'm perfecting my vegan cheese sticks, and I'm thinking we should package those with a delicious dipping sauce. I'm also thinking about vegan cheese fondue kits that include bread and vegetables. And two different kinds of cheese. By the way, how do you feel about vegan aged camembert?" Lucille asked.

Sawyer gripped the wheel as he wove in and out of traffic.

He wanted to take Monty back to his house and never let him out of his sight again. But he couldn't.

Monty seemed happier now as he turned and gazed at Lucille over his shoulder. "Aged camembert, but vegan? It sounds amazing. I've never heard of such a thing." He put his hand on Sawyer's thigh, making him jump. "So far, I'm sure I . . . I . . ." He shook his head.

Lucille had worked sincere magic on Monty. He was blissed out, and Sawyer loved seeing him this way. The last thing he wanted was to let Monty out of the car and for him to walk away. Back into that horrible house. *Man, I hate the thought of him being there. But at least he's safer now the old guy's gone.*

I should be thrilled he remembered this car. It's all coming back to him. Please. Let it happen. He blew out a soft breath as Monty bantered with Lucille.

Sawyer tried to relax as Monty quizzed Lucille on her vegan cheese.

"What brought this idea along?" he asked.

"I think vegans should be allowed to enjoy Thanksgiving without having to feel like all they can eat is a turnip and a handful of carrots," she responded.

"So do I!" Monty seemed so happy.

Sawyer relaxed a little. Lucille was amazing, her excitement infectious. Sawyer wondered when the heck she'd had time to come up with all these culinary creations. And when and how had she developed aged camembert, vegan or otherwise?

"Oh. We're here." Monty sounded disappointed as they arrived at his mom's house.

"We'll pick you up at a quarter to nine," Lucille said as Monty got out of the car.

He nodded, held up a hand in farewell, and ran up the front path.

"Think he'll change his mind and cancel on us?" Sawyer

whispered as Lucille slid into the passenger seat beside him.

"No. I've cocooned him in happy thoughts." She wagged a finger at Sawyer. "You know that little spell only lasts nine and a quarter hours, so we have to be on time in the morning." She pushed back an imaginary loose strand of hair from her forehead. "Which means we have to find that vendor of his super early tomorrow."

"Right." Sawyer waited until Monty had gone inside before turning to her. "Think he'll remember?"

"Yeah. And we need to be ready. I don't think we've heard the last of his old man yet."

Sawyer was about to turn the car around and leave when he spotted a young man with dark hair walking down the street. "Oh, no."

Lucille looked up from her incessant texting. "What?"

"Another victim." Sawyer let out a sigh.

"Call 911. We can't intervene. Wait. I'll do it." She made the call and was put on hold. "Who puts a 911 call on hold?" she screeched. "Holy shit, Sawyer! He's gonna kill him."

She leapt from the car, and Sawyer threw the gears into park, and with the motor still running, made his way to the dark-haired man.

"Run!" Sawyer screamed, but it was too late.

Out of nowhere, a figure shrouded in a hooded cape gained on them. The figure produced a long-bladed knife but didn't pursue the other man. The figure lunged at Sawyer, who ducked in time to miss the knife's thrust. The hooded figure lunged a second time, his face visible for a moment as it twisted in fury.

Sawyer battled the hooded figure as the man who'd been the original target took out a stun gun and fired it into the assailant's back.

The attacker screamed and threw himself around as the gun's crackling sound rang out into the night sky.

Lucille muttered into her phone. "Yes, there's an attack in progress. Hurry. Please. He's got a knife."

The attacker turned on the dark-haired man, who shouted, "LAPD. Drop your weapon, or I'll shoot!"

From out of the house, Monty came running with a shotgun. Sawyer was so shocked, he stared at Monty, then the assailant as he flopped on his side on the ground.

The dark-haired man stepped between them all and cuffed the assailant from behind. He held a gun at the assailant's back.

Sirens blared, and lights blazed as people came running from different directions.

Monty kept staring at the assailant's back as the officers took custody of the prone man.

"Holy crap!" Monty muttered.

"No ID," an officer said.

But Sawyer's concern mounted as Monty's face paled.

"You know this guy?" Sawyer asked.

A couple of the cops looked at Monty.

"Yeah. It's the cheese vendor. The one who took my money then disappeared."

"What's his name?" the arresting officer asked as the uniformed men wrestled with him.

"Tommy de Anzo," Monty responded. "At least, that's what he told me."

"Why did he go after you?" The officer indicated Sawyer.

"No idea. I've never seen him before. We saw — well, Lucille saw him following you, and with all the attacks that have been having on this street —"

"This is an undercover operation," a uniformed officer said. "I'd like your names and addresses, please."

Sawyer, Lucille, and Monty complied. Sawyer worried about Monty's shotgun.

One of the cops pointed at Monty and asked, "Do you have

a permit?"

"No. Don't need one. I live right here. We keep it in the house, but my mom sent me out with it when we realized our friends were in trouble. There was a murder right outside here last night. It was a horrible experience."

"We know," the officer said. "Take it back into the house, please."

Monty nodded and turned on his heel.

De Anzo was still on his side and reached a cuffed hand towards Lucille's ankle, but she put a booted heel on the fake cheese vendor's chest. He let out a yelp, his face contorted in pain and sweat.

The officer turned slitty-eyed. "Whatcha do to him?"

"Nothing." She gave him a tight smile. "He just knows I mean business. I am woman. Hear me roar."

The officer looked nervous. "You seen this guy before?"

She shook her head. "No. But I know an asshole when I see one."

Monty came back outside and stopped dead in his tracks when de Anzo's voice raged.

"I'll fucking kill you. Fuckin' bitch." His voice dropped to a ragged, barely discernible whisper, and uttered what sounded like, "Boo hag."

"You're not killing anyone today," Lucille responded as the arresting officers dragged him to his feet. "Anyway, you'd need to triple-team me." She smiled sweetly.

As the cops dragged de Anzo away, Monty gaped at Lucille. "He knows you're a boo hag?"

She shrugged.

So, Sawyer was right. He *had* called her a boo hag. "Who is he?" he asked.

"Not sure, babe. But I have a feeling a lot of things are starting to fall into place." Lucille glanced at Monty. "Which means all hell is gonna break loose."

Monty gave a nervous laugh. "You make it sound like that's a good thing."

She gave him a radiant smile. "Trust me. It is."

It was hard to let Monty go back inside, but the lingering, longing look he gave Sawyer made him feel all warm and toasty in his very soul. He wasn't sure who Tommy de Anzo really was, but he had an idea. He just didn't know how.

Back in his car and heading home, Sawyer pondered it all.

"He's safe, babe. You're safe. De Anzo's in jail. They're not going to let him go."

"But how did he do it? That's what I want to know." Sawyer's thoughts drifted.

"Well, I'm not sure. He's stronger than we think. Maybe. Anyway, he can't do anything now. His minion's gonna be locked up."

"Think he'll make bail?" The thought made Sawyer desperate.

"No. I don't. This is better than we could have expected."

"Maybe. I still don't feel good leaving Monty and his mom in that house alone."

"They're pretty tough, babe." Lucille chuckled. "Monty's still got that old Winchester."

"Yeah. He does. He seems mighty comfortable with it." Still, Sawyer's chest constricted. He couldn't help feeling bereft at the thought of leaving Monty at the house. "Maybe I should invite him and his mom to stay with me, Lu. What do you think?"

She put a hand on his shoulder, and his body relaxed. "There's time for that, babe. Let it go. Let him be alone with his thoughts tonight. He'll miss you, and tomorrow's another day. I gotta get cooking. Can you floor this thing?"

"I could. But I don't want to be alone."

"Come and watch me cook then."

"Okay." His cell phone rang. It was Monty, sending a text.

Can I come over? Mom took a sleeping pill. She'll be asleep soon.

Sawyer texted back a dozen smile emojis.

Lucille grinned at him. "You dirty, dirty, dirty boys."

Chapter Six

Salad days are here again!

The words tumbled around in Monty's brain as he settled his mom on the sofa with a weighted blanket, the TV remote, and a cup of Cosmic Cocoa. It was a wonderful, soothing concoction he'd discovered at Moon Juice, an eccentric health food store in West Hollywood. All he had to do was mix it with boiling water, and she would relax in an instant. They were almost out of what he'd started thinking of as good goo. He'd buy her more tomorrow.

"Tuck me in?" she whined.

He smiled, thinking that as soon as she was asleep, he'd escape to Sawyer's house. He still couldn't believe he'd texted the guy basically asking for a booty call.

"You're a good boy." His mom seemed relaxed but still a bit tense. The second attack in two nights right outside their door had left her shaken and teary-eyed. "Now leave me to my boys. It's date night, darling."

"Which boys?" He folded the blanket around her body.

He knew she preferred being here all night in command of the TV. She wouldn't sleep in the bedroom. Here, she could see everything going on from the massive windows and the house's open floor plan.

Maybe I shouldn't leave her tonight.

"Briscoe and Curtis." She sipped at her cocoa.

Ah. Briscoe and Curtis. That meant the TV show *Law and Order*. She'd cried like a little girl when actor Jerry Orbach, who'd played Briscoe, had died. Even now, sixteen years later, she'd get weepy when he appeared on camera. The love, the emotion, she rarely showed to her son got transferred to fictional people.

He tried not to think about what had gone on in his bedroom, the one he was back sleeping in. His Grammy frequently gave it a spiritual cleansing, which involved rigorous white soap and bristle brushes and salt left in the corners of the room for up to a week. She would also leave glasses of water by the window and emptied them each day. He never told anybody about this weirdness, but it was very much a part of his life in this house, a big part. He sighed. The water glasses would fill with bubbles, and his Grammy said they were trapping negative energy. He had no idea any of this hooey was true, but it sure felt like it.

God, I miss her. I hope she comes home soon.

"Go and have fun." His mom turned up the volume and fixed her loving gaze on her boys.

Dismissed.

"I can text you if I need you. You have no idea how much I've wanted to have a night alone with the TV. I love you, babe, but you don't need to babysit me. We got any ice cream?"

"I think so."

In the kitchen, he found a pint of supermarket-brand pecan praline, lurking in the back with a couple of frozen dinners. Not her favorite, but he couldn't keep the good stuff in the freezer long enough. He opened the container and worked to make the contents soupy. By the time he returned to the living room, she was asleep.

Monty left the TV on, the remote on the coffee table, and took the ice cream back to the freezer.

Salad days are here again!

There were those words again. He sighed, leaning against the counter, and Googled them on his cell phone. Huh. A Procol Harum song from 1967. He clicked the YouTube link and played it. The album cover seemed familiar, but he didn't know why. It was a black and white pencil drawing of a beautiful woman with long, flowing, curly hair with tree branches around her, and a long white dress—the ultimate hippie child, at one with nature. Oddly, he knew all the lyrics to the songs but had no idea why. Or why it affected him so much.

How do I know these words? I've never even heard of Procol Harum. And yet, the album cover hurt his heart. *I'm so happy to see it again.* Why? Tears coursed down his cheeks. It made him think of one of his mom's dippy sayings. *Happy as a dead pig in sunshine.*

A fleeting thought flashed through his mind of a rainy afternoon, locked in his bedroom. Not this one. The other one. The other house. The other life. He had three albums. His breath caught as he watched himself playing Simon and Garfunkel's *Parsley, Sage, Rosemary and Thyme* on his record player. Tears blinded the memories of singing along with *Scarborough Fair.*

I was happy then. Why did it end?

Then he saw the Procol Harum album and The Beatles' *Magical Mystery Tour.* He laughed through his tears, remembering his parents going nuts when he played *Penny Lane* repeatedly.

His mind went blank.

Monty blew out a breath. Time for a shower, then an Uber over to Sawyer's. He let Procol Harum's *Whiter Shade of Pale* album play on his phone as he showered and changed. He knew the lyrics of all the songs. *How? Why?* He called an Uber, feeling excited yet strange.

How do I know Sawyer?

He chose his clothing more carefully than usual. His ex, Luke, once described Monty's ad-hoc dress style as a *multiple vehicle collision.* Monty always thought that was funny. Now, as his gaze fell on the pricey Buttercloth brand Tulum shirt his mom had given him for Christmas, he was sorry he didn't put more effort into what he wore. He pulled the shirt out, studying it. Happily unworn, it was therefore clean and presentable. The fabric was the softest, most luxurious thing he'd ever touched. He'd proclaimed it too nice to ever wear it for daily use.

Tonight's the night.

Monty loved the shirt. The pale but vibrant blue made him think of Sawyer's eyes. *Yeah. I'll wear it with jeans and boots.* He dressed and called for an Uber X, which arrived six minutes later. Eight minutes after he got in, the vehicle approached Sawyer's home. The garage door popped open as if by osmosis. As it rose, Sawyer stepped out in a faint halo of shadow. He was so magnificent, Monty's breath caught in his throat.

Monty's Uber driver said something, but he would never know what it was. Monty's gazed fixed on Sawyer, and he was in his arms in his garage seconds later. The intoxicating smell of Sawyer's soap mixed with enticing scents of garlic and lemon from the kitchen made Monty's pulse race.

Sawyer looked so handsome and happy, coming into the garage to greet him. Monty took in the white silk shirt tucked into tight black jeans and Sawyer's bare feet. He was like a sex god from the cover of a romance novel. Monty's cock hardened in response. *Oh, God. This man owns me.*

Sawyer glanced down, a predatory gleam in his eyes as he ran a hand across the pull of Monty's crotch and kissed him deeply. It was no mere greeting, but a kiss with serious intent. As Sawyer held him close, Monty ran his hands over Sawyer's toned back and arms, sighing with pleasure at the feel of the taut ass cheeks now in his firm grip. Monty pressed himself against Sawyer and undid one of his shirt buttons, revealing a little of what seemed to be a perfect torso.

Monty couldn't help but feel a small thrill since Sawyer hadn't allowed him much access to him during their last encounter. He worked to undo one more button, delighted when he glimpsed a hint of an exquisitely cut six-pack. Monty bit his lip and popped another button, leaving the rest to disappear into Sawyer's waistband.

Sawyer dropped a kiss on Monty's cheek. "You're going to have to take my shirt out. I'm as hard as hell for you, baby."

"Yeah, you are, aren't you?" Monty pulled at Sawyer's shirt, and a button flew off, bouncing to the ground. Soft, almost sheer folds of expensive silk fell over Sawyer's beautiful, flat belly. Monty let his hand loiter over the bulky package in Sawyer's pants. Sawyer smirked, giving him another kiss.

"What happened to us?" Monty asked.

Sawyer took Monty's face in his hands, his eyes flooding with the darkness of pain and anguish. "Let's talk about that later. Come on, I've . . . we've both waited too long for this."

He took Monty's hand and pulled him into the house. He used his remote to lower the garage door. With a jolt, Monty realized it had been open the whole time they'd been mauling each other.

"I like a live sex show as much as the next guy, but I want you to myself now." Sawyer kissed Monty's chin then kick-shut the door leading into the house, locking it. He moved his mouth across Monty's jawline, slamming him against the first wall they came to, his tongue at Monty's throat.

"Fuck me. Oh, fuck me," Monty begged.

Sawyer ignored him, tonguing around the space between Monty's throat and the buttoned-down shirt he wore. "Nice. I'll try not to rip it to shreds." He undid a couple of buttons and stared into Monty's eyes. "I might want to wear this one day. The color matches my eyes, don't you think?"

Monty's temperature soared as Sawyer ran his fingers underneath the smooth fabric then lifted the shirt, licking Monty's nipples to erect attention. Monty remembered something. *What?* A fragment of recall. This same moment of exquisite pleasure, then . . . a black cloud. For a moment, wild panic enveloped him.

Sawyer raised his face from Monty's chest. "Don't think of it. Not now. Don't let them win."

Monty wanted to ask *Who?*, but Sawyer was unbuttoning Monty's jeans. The black clouds rolled out of his mind, and the feeling of wanting Sawyer to touch him urgently was all that mattered.

Sawyer took Monty's chin in his thumb and forefinger. "I don't have rubbers in the nightstand or anything like that. I'm not prepared. I haven't been with anyone since you. There was never anyone but you."

"I'm prepared." Monty reached into his rear pocket and pulled out his wallet. "My emergency condom."

For a moment, Sawyer seemed disappointed. Then he smiled. "And this is an emergency?"

"Fuck, yes. I haven't been with anyone since I broke up with my boyfriend, Luke."

Sawyer's eyes filled with pain. It was such an immense sensation that Monty felt it, even mirrored it, and regretted not knowing their past.

"I know." Sawyer gave him a small, sad smile. "Come on. Let's not waste any more time."

"How long has it been for us?" Monty asked. He unzipped Sawyer's pants and dug inside for the enormous cock he knew awaited him. He pulled it out, over the top of his pants. He was commando. *Oh, boy.* He had one delicious cock that sprang to attention the second Monty's fingers closed around the shaft.

Sawyer moaned. "A lifetime."

His response didn't surprise Monty, but it also didn't reveal much. He marveled at how well he was navigating these unknown waters so well. *Am I crazy?*

"Somebody's in a big rush," Sawyer murmured.

Monty grinned as their gazes filled with helpless lust

overtaking them. "How many years has it been?"

Sawyer said nothing.

"This is the most beautiful cock in the world, Sawyer."

Monty leaned into him, Sawyer's entrapped shaft between them. They exchanged more heated kisses and ignited some distant, dark but enticing memory that vanished like a puff of smoke. He was still holding Sawyer in his hot grip when Sawyer grabbed his hand and led him down the hall. It made for awkward walking yet total joy as they returned to the bedroom, the scene of their earlier sex crimes, and they fell in an ecstatic heap on the bed.

They tugged at each other's clothes, Sawyer curling his hand around Monty's shaft. He seemed to take such pleasure out of licking and sucking the length that Monty wanted to let him continue. But he couldn't. He had needs, too. He buried his hands in Sawyer's hair for a moment then reached down for his balls, which seemed to react to the attention they so richly deserved. Monty let his hand slip deeper and his fingers connected with Sawyer's ass.

Sawyer pushed him away for a moment, burying his face in Monty's ass, licking all the way up to the length of his shaft like a cat scraping the bowl for last dregs of fresh cream.

Monty hollered out his pleasure, not realizing it until Sawyer lifted his face, glossy with Monty's juices, and laughed.

"I'd forgotten what a noisy, active lover you are." He placed a kiss on Monty's inner thigh.

Monty panted. "Yeah? I don't remember. When was that?"

Sawyer responded by rolling Monty over onto his belly, stroking his neck, back, and thighs. He put some more hot licks onto Monty's ass, and after slipping on the rubber, wasted not a second more getting that huge cock into him. Their bodies shook with the impact of shared bliss.

Monty hung onto the bedding with his hands and knees as Sawyer fucked him with impassioned intent. He matched

Monty's thrusts and grunts as he continued his full-tilt plunges until he exploded deep within him. Monty came at the same moment he did, all over the bedspread.

Sawyer paused a moment as they luxuriated in their wild ride. Then he lifted Monty up, threw down the covers, and put him on his back on the bed. He opened Monty's thighs and went down on Monty's ass . . . again.

Monty moaned. He couldn't wait to regain possession of that perfect cock inside him, but they were out of love gloves, and Sawyer seemed content to leave Monty wanting more.

They exchanged heated kisses until Monty's desire mounted again.

"Rest now," Sawyer murmured. "Sleep in my arms, the way you were meant to."

This is My Song. Monty awakened around three a.m., the song dancing around in his head. It took a moment for him to realize it was because it was on the radio.

"We have to go," Sawyer said, reaching over to kiss him.

"Go? Go where? And why do I know this song?" Monty stared at the radio. "I think I used to love this song, but I don't remember it." He pulled his cell phone from the nightstand. "Who's singing this?"

"I believe it's Engelbert Humperdinck but—"

"This song used to make me so happy." Monty sang along with the tune as he Googled it. "Written by Charlie Chaplin of all people. For Petula Clark."

The song was released in *1967.*

"Why is 1967 significant to us?" The words tumbled fast before Monty could stop them. "I'm remembering songs, whole songs I never knew before. Everything points to that year. Why? What the hell happened to us?"

Sawyer sat up in bed, closing his eyes as he leaned forward and swayed a little. "That's the year your father tried to kill you."

Monty stared at him. "But I wasn't even born yet!"

Sawyer said nothing, keeping his head down.

"So, he didn't kill me?" He shook his head. "What am I saying? This is *insane*."

"Not insane. Mentally challenging, maybe." Sawyer never glanced up but slowly shook his head. "I made him take me instead."

"What?"

Sawyer wouldn't, *couldn't* explain more, but the words were out, and with them, a terrible weight shed from his skin and soul. It was as though he'd been pressed against a gigantic boulder he'd been holding and couldn't put anywhere. *Let the chips fall where they may.*

"What did my disgusting father do to you?"

"It doesn't matter now."

"Are you . . . are you okay?" Monty stared at him, his eyes wide with shock.

"You'll remember, my love." Sawyer's whole body contorted in grief.

"I love you." Monty's eyes brimmed with tears, clearly teetering on the edge of the truth.

"I love you, too." He took Monty's hand, a part of him floating above, watching the scene. How many times in the past decades, past their *salad days*, had he watched Monty from above? So close and yet miles and miles away from him. Just to be able to touch him was a blessing — a sheer miracle.

"Please. I want you to come to my house for Thanksgiving," Monty blurted.

Yes! Oh, my God. He said it. He did it! "I would love that." Sawyer tried to sound a lot more casual than he felt.

"My grandmother is cooking. She makes weird stuff, but it's mostly edible." Monty's nervous laugh was warranted.

Sawyer remembered the old lady and knew her food well. He didn't care what she made. She could stick a live frog on a plate, and he'd figure out how to eat it. *I sure hope not, though. I hope her kitchen skills have improved some.* He couldn't resist a smile.

"Is that a yes?"

Sawyer nodded. "Of course, it's a yes!" *Oh, man. I hope she doesn't make her crazy Coke salad anymore . . .*

"Great. Now, why are we going back to work so early?"

Sawyer realized in that moment that Monty was accepting everything so well because he was still under Lucille's love spell. Seconds later, it seemed to wear off.

"I have a headache, like I'm hungover." Monty clutched his head.

Yeah, the spell often had that side effect. "You need coffee." Sawyer swung his feet over the side of the bed. "I have to chuck out all last night's food since we skipped dinner and it's all still sitting on the stove, but I can rustle up some coffee and maybe a slice of toast."

"You're avoiding my question. Why are we going to work so early?"

"We need to prepare for business today."

"Oh." Monty looked confused for a moment. "Is it going to be as insanely busy today as it was yesterday?"

Sawyer winced. "Probably more so."

"Let's get going then. I do want that coffee, though. Maybe two." He clutched Sawyer's arm. "You may wanna rethink my Thanksgiving invitation. My grandmother makes some pretty weird stuff."

Tell me about it. "Does she still make polk salad?"

Monty's jaw dropped. "Wait. You know my Grammy's cooking? Now you're freaking me out."

Sawyer laughed. "Oh, *now* I'm freaking you out?" He leaned over and kissed him. "I can't wait for Thanksgiving dinner." It occurred to him that he hadn't asked Monty if she still made potato candy, but his stomach was already in knots at the prospect of that sweet old lady's food.

Half an hour later, Sawyer dropped Monty outside The Cheese Guy and zoomed into one of the Beverly Hills city parking lots. He hated letting Monty out of his sight, but Lucille was on her way with heavy containers. Besides, Sawyer was certain Freddie Piano was lurking nearby, keeping a protective eye on him.

Sawyer covered the few blocks to the store in a couple of minutes, relishing in the dark calm of the neighborhood. *While the city sleeps.* He thought about how close he and Monty had become again in such a short time —

Freddie.

Ugh.

It was hard not to feel jealous of Monty's self-appointed guardian angel. It was clear to Sawyer that Monty didn't recognize Freddie from their, er, earlier life together. To atone for his terrible sins against him, Freddie had chosen to avoid an early death by looking after Monty. *I know he's straight and married and has a bunch of children, but Monty is drawn to him. He just doesn't know why.*

Monty was inside the store, drinking coffee with Freddie. The youngest Piano, Hamish, was there too, drinking hot coffee through a straw. Perched on the countertop beside his dad, Hamish looked happy. The kid always looked happy. Freddie must have been doing a bang-up job making amends for his past transgressions. Because he was a rare guardian, who'd been given the unusual privilege of being allowed to have children and an outwardly normal life.

Hamish gave Sawyer a toothy grin. Because of his inherited magical abilities, Hamish and his siblings aged faster than most *human* kids. They, too, possessed Freddie's supernatural talents. They could also tune pianos already, giving them the perfect, mundane cover as they grew older. The fact that they could also split a human head open like a watermelon was just by the by.

"Hello, Soy," Hamish said. It was hard to feel churlish when Hamish had a nickname for him. "Did you see the new cheese?" He dipped his head to the straw again.

What the heck was he talking about? Sawyer glanced around, then he spotted it. Today's new culinary creation in the window. Damned breathtaking.

"Wow. It's a cornucopia, right?" Sawyer moved toward it, accepting the cup of coffee Monty handed him. With a jolt, he realized it was a Tiffany cup, made with the company's trademark blue. Some might have called it haint blue. He felt nothing but the simple joy of a delicious cup of coffee as he sipped at it, enjoying the splendor of Lucille's latest creation.

"She's really good at this," Sawyer said, hardly able to believe the wonder of the horn-shaped cheese on an enormous platter. The *horn of plenty* was the symbol of abundance, and by definition, Thanksgiving. He marveled at the array of harvest fruit and vegetables tumbling out of the horn. Pumpkins, squash, grapes, apples, and a dusting of autumn leaves completed the display. All appeared to be made of cheese with delicate coloring.

"Don't sound so surprised." Lucille slapped Sawyer's arm playfully.

"How did you get the colors into the cheese?" he asked, mesmerized. "It makes me hungry."

"Organic food coloring."

"Amazing. And what happened to the Magic School Bus?"

"We're donating it to the Children's Hospital. I was just wrapping it in the back. Want to try today's samples?"

Sawyer couldn't get over her transformation. "We don't deserve you," he whispered.

She winked. "You don't, but he does." She pointed at Monty, who watched them from behind the counter. She gestured to Sawyer. "Come on, you can help me pack the dry ice."

He followed her to the kitchen, where stacks of plastic containers lay on the countertop.

"I outdid myself today." She clapped her hands together. A moment later, two women appeared at the backdoor.

"Did you leave this open?" Lucille asked Sawyer before swiveling her attention to the two women.

"No. I haven't been back here." Sawyer watched them, a weird feeling coming over him. There was something strange about them. Clad in brown skirts, jackets, and black, buckled shoes, they had mean little eyes, and their gazes flickered everywhere.

"Can we come in?" one of them asked.

"It's four-thirty in the morning." Lucille sounded exasperated. "We're not open yet."

"We're from the Health and Safety Commission for the city of Beverly Hills," the second woman said.

"The Health and Safety Commission?" Lucille squinted at the badge the first woman flashed at her. "May I see that, please?"

She didn't produce it a second time. "We've had a complaint."

"A complaint?" Sawyer echoed. "Who from?"

"I'd still like to see your badge. I know my rights, and unless I see a piece of paper, and I get a closer look at your credentials, you're not coming in here."

"We'd like to come in." The second woman focused on Lucille, whose face flushed with fury.

"I am not inviting you in."

The hairs on the back of Sawyer's neck stood up. There was something off about these two. Way off.

"Who are you, really?" He stood beside Lucille

The first woman seemed nervous, but the second one held

firm. "We just told you. We're from the Health and Safety Commission—"

"Yeah, yeah. And you make a habit of descending on people before sunrise. What was the nature of this complaint?" Lucille blocked the women's entry into the kitchen.

"We're here on official business." The second woman looked frightened now.

"No, you're not. What are you up to?" Lucille stood, hands on hips, staring them down.

The women backed away.

"We'll be back," the second woman said.

"I want your names," Lucille insisted, but the two women left the store.

"Who do you think they were?" Sawyer asked Lucille. "I sensed no supernatural interference."

"You didn't?" She seemed pleased.

"Why are you smiling? You mean you do? And I don't? Am I losing my touch?"

She gave him a swift hug. "Oh, my dear, this is such good news. It means you're becoming more human."

"Okay." He liked that idea, but he'd somehow forgotten that reintegration with Monty would mean he'd lose all touch with the infinite. He felt like the Lady of Shallot, cursed to look at the world through a mirror. He, like she, was half-sick of shadows but feared being human would rob him of the ability to protect the man he loved. "So, tell me, who are they?"

"Not who, *what*." Lucille rocked on her toes. "They're drugstore beetles."

"Who the hell sent them here?" Sawyer wanted to knock somebody's block off. He'd heard of evil humans sending dreaded insects in human form to people's homes and businesses but had never seen them in action before. From what he understood, they would enter food sources and could even demolish books and rolls of aluminum foil. If a real health inspector showed up and found an infestation of the pesky critters, poor Monty would be shut down for days, maybe even weeks.

Drugstore beetles were hard to detect and even harder to eliminate because they could hide anywhere and could survive for weeks without food.

"They're an old-fashioned style insect, right?" Sawyer asked, thinking out loud.

"Right. Haven't seen 'em around much." Lucille closed and locked the backdoor. "Who hates Monty enough to see his business suffer?" She looked even more pale than usual.

"The realtor, for one." Sawyer's thoughts raced. "She seems very interested in his store being a failure."

"Right. I wonder who put her up to it. I don't think it's her." Lucille snapped her fingers. "She mentioned she had a buyer."

"What about the cheese vendor? Is he still in jail?"

"Haven't checked." Lucille's cheeks flushed crimson. "We need to be vigilant. Somebody doesn't want to see him do well. Any idea who looted his place a few weeks ago?"

"No idea." Sawyer's frustration mounted. "That sounded like a personal attack. Maybe it's the same person who sent the realtor here. I still think Donna Harridan might be involved."

Lucille smiled finally. "Harrigan. Harridan suits her, though." Suddenly she screeched, "Freddie!"

Freddie came in seconds later and sniffed. "I smell beetles. Why?"

Lucille and Sawyer explained what had just happened, and his brows met as his face took on a mask of total rage.

"You should have called me right away. I love squashing beetles." He wagged a finger at them, then cracked his knuckles. It sounded like thunder erupting in the kitchen. "Let me handle this. And keep this door locked."

"We will." Lucille looked anxious.

Sawyer felt terrible for her. With his paranormal powers slipping away, she was on her own . . . with the Piano man.

Freddie strode back out to the shop, bawling for Hamish to follow him.

Monty came into the kitchen. "What's going on? What did I miss?"

Lucille put a hand on Sawyer's arm. "He's losing his powers, Monty. He's not going to be able to flit between two worlds soon, but somebody who has a foot in each is trying to destroy you."

Monty swayed then recovered himself. As Lucille and Sawyer explained what had happened, he stared at them, incredulous.

"I cannot have drugstore beetles back in here," he said, his voice a loud roar.

Lucille and Sawyer exchanged looks.

"You've already had them here?" she asked.

"Yes." Monty ran a hand over his face. "The cheese vendor. He first came here before the looting happened. The Health and Safety Commission showed up while he was here. Next thing I knew, I had these ugly beetles everywhere. I'd never seen them before. The health department made me close the shop and put a poor health grade sticker on the window. It was horrible. That night, my store was looted. Practically destroyed." He lapsed into silence. "It's weird, you know. Those beetles disappeared after that, but I still had the place fumigated, just in case."

For long moments, they all looked at each other.

"Somebody really has it in for me." Monty sounded miserable.

"Any idea who?" Sawyer reached for him, but Monty held back.

"I know it's him. I just don't know how he's doing it."

"Who?" Sawyer asked.

"Only one person hates me enough to ruin me like this. My father."

CHAPTER SEVEN

Around eight o'clock, Monty checked on his dad, relieved to learn he was still in his room inside the assisted living facility.

"He had a rough night," the head nurse reported. "He's been sedated since midnight."

"Any chance he can escape?" Monty tried not to fret about this possibility.

"Not at all." The nurse hesitated. "Your mom just called and asked me the same thing. I want you to be assured he's in our special memory care facility. We have an excellent team working around the clock to assist our patients. He has been showing an increase in confusion and agitation the last few days, so we've worked on his enrichment programs and whole brain fitness regime. He's responded well, but he requires a lot of supervision."

"So how did he get out last night?"

"He's been very restless. He suffers severely from sundowning, which is—"

"I know what it is." Monty knew his father had a bad case of sleeplessness and a relentless rage from dusk to dawn. It had been impossible for his mother to handle his father's terrifying behavior late into the night.

The nurse went on. "One of our orderlies, a new one, made the mistake of taking your father out in a wheelchair for fresh air last night, not realizing he was completely mobile and capable of strolling out of here. It's a mistake that won't be repeated, I promise you."

"How about the rages?"

"Responding well to medicine. We've tried a few. It hasn't been easy. Right now, he's on *Abilify*, which seems to be helping him sleep. Last night he received an injection of clozapine, which helped tremendously with his aggression and ah, hallucinations."

Hallucinations. Monty tried not to think about his father's behavior in the alleyway. It was heartbreaking to know he hated Sawyer so much.

"Okay, thanks." Monty ended the call, trying not to think about the horrible expression on his father's face when he'd encountered him in the alley. *How does he know Sawyer is here?* His thoughts flickered to the mysterious women posing as health officials.

Who the hell sent them?

He couldn't dwell. He and his small but mighty crew had to get everything ready for another busy day.

"We haven't discussed wages," he said, feelings of guilt washing over him.

"Shut up!" Lucille and Sawyer said in unison.

He laughed. "I mean it."

"Shut up!" they said again.

Monty wondered how he'd ever gotten through a day without these two. He'd never had friends like them. He glanced at Sawyer, wondering how long they'd been apart. *Did my father really kill him? And yet here he is. Impossible.*

He brushed the thoughts aside as they worked in companionable silence, Lucille sweeping and mopping the floors for the seventh, or was it eighth time?

Around eight-thirty, Monty got a text from his former cheese queen, Rima.

How's it going? Heard you reopened. Do you have the recipe for cheese straws? Mine isn't working.

He archived the text, blocking her number. He wouldn't give her the recipe for anything. He couldn't help feeling a little smug as he set up the day's samples. She'd never done half the work Lucille had. He cast a fond glance in Lu's direction as she made sure there were disposable cups, gloves, tiny forks, and plenty of hand sanitizer.

"I think I should clean the window again." She said this to herself more than anyone else, it seemed, and raced outside in her impossibly high shoes. She made him feel everything was going to be fine.

Sawyer came over and gave him a kiss.

"Please don't worry," he whispered against Monty's lips. "We have your back."

Yes. Monty believed everything would be great. Still, he fretted as they organized everything, replenishing missing stock and adding new flavors of packaged mixes. He had to be vigilant. He couldn't have everybody's hard work wrecked by his father — or anyone else's devious activities.

He called his mother a little before nine. She said she was on her way to visit his dad at the care facility.

"He's having an episode again." She sighed. "They're talking about giving him risperidone, which could help him, but it can be risky. I'm willing to let them try. I'm heading over there now to sign the consent forms. They tell me his new girlfriend can't handle his moods." She gave a nasty laugh. "I told them, welcome to my world."

"Want me to come with you?" He hoped with his whole heart that she'd say no.

"No way. You stay where you are. I'll pop by the store on my way home and see how everything looks. I saw the photos on Instagram. It looks amazing!"

Instagram? Monty almost laughed. That had to be Lucille's handiwork. It wouldn't have occurred to him to do it. *Ah, that's how Rima knows where back in business.*

He made sure to put a fresh batch of cheese straws in the display case. *I'll ask Lu to post these as well.*

At last, with customers lined up out front, they opened on

the dot of nine. Monty noticed Freddie Piano lurking across the road, watching the shop. He gave Monty a thumbs up. Monty returned the gesture, his stomach twisting in anguish.

He hardly had time to think about anything else except business until eleven o'clock when the doctor's office kitty-corner to his store called and asked for a delivery of four cheese salads.

"They're almost ready," Lucille said.

Monty couldn't believe it. "How did you know?"

"You didn't hire me for my eclectic wardrobe, babe. Want me to walk them over?"

"I'll do it. You should take a break."

"Don't mind if I do. There are six cheeses in three of them, seven in the one with the lid marked B, for blue cheese. I think I'll make a quick coffee. Want one? I can have it ready for you when you return."

"Sure. Thanks." He finished packing the delivery bags with napkins, forks, the sample bag of cheese straws Lucille handed him, and takeout menus.

He stopped by the counter where Sawyer was sharing a joke with a female customer. He and Monty exchanged searing looks, then as he stepped outside, a little Piano approached him.

"Me dad said I should take the salads. You should stay 'ere."

Why did the kid sound like something out of a Jason Statham north London gangster movie?

"People will think I've hired slave labor if I send a child over there," Monty said.

"Oy. Who you callin' a child?" The kid looked like he might throw a punch any second.

"Ask Lucille to make you a coffee. She likes you," Monty blurted.

"She does? All right then. Whatever you do. Avoid the

park." The kid touched his nose and brushed past Monty.

"I had no plans to go anywhere near the—Okay. I will." Monty waited until the kid had gone inside, feeling a little bad that he'd sicked him onto Lu. *She's a big girl. She can handle herself. I hope.* He thought about texting her with a warning, but his hands were full with the delivery bags.

Naturally, being told not to go near the park, he had to do it. He dropped off the salads at the business office where the assistant handed him a dollar bill for a tip—last of the big spenders. Then he detoured past the small patch of green where Beverly Hills mothers and nannies used to entertain their little darlings.

Monty was startled to see Donna Harridan squeezed onto a tiny swing set. She was pushing herself high above the sand-pit, screaming *Wheeee!* in total delight as she rose higher and higher. More than a few adults frowned, and kids watched in mounting dismay. One kid was even crying. Nobody likes a playground hog. Especially an adult keeping a child-size swing hostage.

Donna seemed oblivious as she screeched with joy. She was obviously not of sound mind.

What the hell did Freddie do to her?

At one point, she rose so high above the top of the swings, onlookers gasped, but Donna just laughed and laughed as first her shoes, then her pearls flew off onto the grass beyond the sandpit. The swing's posts wobbled, but Donna pushed on, almost flying right off the swing seat.

Monty knew the moms would start yelling since it was a kids' play area, so he did the only sensible thing. He turned around and went back to the store.

The shop seemed devoid of customers for the moment. And judging by the looks of things, Lucille and Sawyer were busy straightening store merchandise from the recent on-slaught.

"What took you so long? My lips are getting cold." Sawyer

frowned then kissed him. "You went by the swings. Didn't Hamish tell you not to go there?"

"The little guy? Is that his name? Yeah. He did, but I've never liked being told what to do."

Sawyer's facial expression softened. "It's one of the things I love most about you. Here, you haven't tried today's special yet. Vegan cream cheese apple cinnamon rolls."

"You don't say?" Monty took the sample cup and removed the gooey wedge with his fingertips. A few seconds later, his soul went into orbit. "This is amazing."

Lucille, who was busy straightening items on the shelves, turned and gave him a huge grin. "Glad you like it. We've almost sold out of the kits."

"Kits?" Monty raised a brow in her direction. "Save one for me, will you?"

Her smile widened. "Anything for you, chief."

Seconds later, two men walked into the store. Monty recognized one of them as Steven Shields, the insurance adjuster who'd come in to appraise the premises after it had been looted and damaged.

Shields glanced around. "Looks much better than the last time I saw this place."

"Doesn't it?" Monty tried to relax, but it was hard.

"Mr. Pellman—"

"Monty, please."

Shields gave a little grimace, which told Monty this wasn't a social visit.

Monty tried to keep things polite, at least. "Steven Shields, let me introduce my co-workers, Lucille and Sawyer."

They nodded to Shields, who held a ten-inch electronic tablet in his hands.

"This is, ah, Tony Brandon. He's a forensic fraud examiner." Shields avoided looking him in the eye.

Last time they'd seen each other, Shields had hit on him.

"A what?" Monty couldn't believe what he was hearing.

"We obtained some footage from the day, or rather the evening of the, er, incident."

"I thought there wasn't any." Monty panicked. "The police couldn't find any, and you said you couldn't—"

"Evidence was turned over to us." Shields tapped the screen and turned it around for him to watch.

Monty was stunned to see two people attacking his store. Out front, a luxury SUV loitered. A man in a monkey mask sat behind the wheel while two people broke into the store.

Monty stared, incredulous.

"You recognize them?" Shields asked.

Monty could barely speak over the lump in his throat. "I think one of them is Donna Harrigan. I'm almost certain it is."

"She just confessed. She took a fall in the Beverly Hills park and insisted on speaking to the police. This footage is from her phone."

Monty squinted at it. He caught a glimpse of a third figure who glanced into the store then scuttled away. He said nothing about this person since they didn't appear to be a part of the assault. Monty recognized her though and wondered why she'd run off, smiling.

"Do you recognize the second person with the sledgehammer?" Tony Brandon spoke at last.

"I think it's my former chef, Rima."

"She's Harrigan's daughter. Harrigan admits they sabotaged you because she wanted her daughter to take over this location."

Monty watched the footage a second time. "I had no idea."

He hardly heard what the two men said after that. He kept replaying the scene in his mind. Suddenly, things came back to him. Things he'd locked deep in his soul that wanted to remain hidden, dormant. Things that had caused so much pain and violence.

He did hear Lucille tell the investigating officers that Rima had called a couple of times that day, pretending to be different customers, asking for the recipe for cheese straws. Shields and Brandon tried samples, their faces taking on looks of bliss as they ate them.

"I'm sorry I thought you were involved in this." Shields looked embarrassed.

Monty said nothing. He had been devastated that the insurance company had stalled on giving him compensation, saying they were still investigating his claim. But it made sense now. He'd had to take out a loan against his condo to reopen.

"We will absolve you of any wrongdoing, and we'll rectify the payment issue immediately, Mr. Pellman." Shields held his gaze for a moment.

But Monty didn't care about money. He didn't care about anything except saving the man he loved. He waited until Brandon and Shields have left before turning to his friends.

"I'm starting to remember. I have no idea why, but my mother was here when the attack took place." He stopped. "I think she wanted them to demolish the haint." He closed his eyes. "Sawyer, can you take me home? Lucille, please. We need to lock up. You need to be there."

"Of course," she said, just as a group of customers descended on them.

"Family emergency," Lucille told them, pressing free cream cheese cinnamon bun kits into their hands. "So sorry!"

Sawyer led Monty away from the store.

Flashes of memories came back to Monty. None of them good.

"Hang in there," Sawyer urged, putting his arm around Monty.

In the parking lot, they climbed into the car. Monty wept as he Googled Tucker Pellman, Charleston, South Carolina,

1967.

It was a good thing he wasn't driving. He couldn't believe the words that now swam before his eyes as he read a small article in the North Charleston Banner dated November 1967.

Fatal Thanksgiving Accident on U.S Coastal Highway 17

Charleston police department say a single-car accident resulted in a fatal collision off the highway yesterday, Thursday, November 23. Authorities say lightning caused by a freak storm hit the car, which ran off the road, rolling twice before colliding with a barn. Both passenger and driver were killed on impact. Tucker Montgomery Pellman, 18, and Dillon Sawyer, 19, both perished in the crash. Both men's bodies were burned in the wreckage. Only Pellman's body was able to be identified.

Monty read and re-read the small column. Dillon Sawyer. He'd hated his first name. Always. He only ever went by Sawyer. The events of that dreadful night seared into his brain.

Oh, God. I remember. He squeezed his eyes shut, but it only made the memories more vivid. There'd been no car. No accident.

It had been murder. And yeah. There had been lightning. And thunder.

And death.

"Oh, Sawyer."

Sawyer reached across the seat for his hand.

"It's time to kill the moon." Monty hung his head, hoping he was strong enough to smash this horrible curse.

If I find that damned moon.

"Do you remember what he did with the moon?"

Sawyer was surprised to hear Lucille's voice coming from the backseat. He couldn't remember her being in the car, but he was grateful she was here. He—they—needed her.

At Monty's house, all three of them walked to the front door. Monty clutched their hands. Sawyer knew that Monty remembered. He could feel it with the vibration of his whole being.

Monty's mother opened the door, and her face became wreathed in smiles when she saw them.

"Oh, Dillon. Oh, my boy. I can't believe you're here." She threw herself at him and held him, burying her face in his chest. Her tears, which seem to pour from her very soul, soaked his chest. At last, she pulled herself away from him and turned her gaze to Monty. "Son, aren't you going to welcome our guest inside?"

He stared at her, then tore his gaze away to glance at Sawyer. "Of course." He smiled through shaky lips and blurred eyes. "Please come in."

He pulled Sawyer and Lucille across the threshold. The day suddenly flashed into darkness. Lightning cracked above the house.

"Hurry." Monty was worried. He had no idea how long he had to rectify this terrible wrong but only wished—

"Bathilde!" he gasped after turning to look at Lucille. He hugged her hard with one arm, his other still holding onto Sawyer.

"You never guessed it was me?"

"No. Never. And I thought you were a bad boo."

"I can be bad on occasion."

Sawyer loved watching them reconnect. It had been hard not telling Monty that Lucille was his beloved traiteur, but the secret was out now.

In the hallway, Monty stared at the wedding photo of his mother. "I finally understand why this photo has always bothered me. It wasn't taken in 1967. Was it, Mom?" He glanced at her.

Her shoulders sagged, and with a low moan, she whispered, "No."

"I don't know how many times I've seen this photo and never really looked at it properly. Mom, what is that crown you're wearing? Are you a queen of some kind?"

She looked stunned. In Sawyer's whole life, and times in between, he never expected her to tell him the truth.

"A voodoo queen. It's your father who has all the power. Mine is in name only. He's a voodoo king. Well, he was. After what he did to you and Sawyer, we were excommunicated."

Monty stared at her. "When was this photo taken? When were you married?"

"1948." A long silence then, "I had a photographer retouch the photo trying to streamline the dress a little. You'd laugh if you could see the original."

Monty asked, "Laugh? So far, I don't find any of this funny. Mom, when was I born?"

"1949."

"*1949*? That means I must be what, 57 years old?"

"Your father was able to stop time."

"I can't be almost sixty! That's impossible."

"No. It's not." Monty's mom rubbed at her sweaty brow. "He sent you back to being a baby and banished Sawyer away from you. You were in love, and he stopped your relationship."

Sawyer put a supporting hand on Monty's shoulder as she said this.

Monty turned to him. "Where did he send you?"

"He trapped my spirit in a moon-shaped haint. It's here somewhere. All this time, we've waited for your father to lose his grip on reality or die. Whichever came first. Lucille, or Bathilde, she's been with me, and with you the whole time. She chose to be our protector, but until your father voluntarily left this house, she couldn't help bring me back to your world."

"Is this for real?" Monty covered Sawyer's hand with his. He'd done that and more many times since Sawyer had returned to him.

"Yes. But, unless we find the moon by the end of Thanksgiving, I may die altogether. I'll be gone for good."

"Don't say that," Monty insisted. "We'll find it." He turned to his mom, lashing out at her. "Why did you stay with my father after all of that? He's a monster!"

Her face flushed. "I got to do what no other mother in the world got to do. He gave me back my baby. I got to raise you up again and enjoy your babyhood once more. Do you know how many mothers mourn their children growing up and growing away from them?"

Monty just stared at her.

Sawyer was surprised it meant that to her, but then again, he knew she loved her son. He knew it cost her dearly when Monty fled the house after he'd been locked up in it for months.

"Do we know for sure the moon glass is here?" Monty asked, sounding exhausted.

"Yes." Sawyer waved a hand around. "I can never be too far away from the house. It's never left here. It was only when your father left this house that I was able to go get the house in Beverly Hills."

"He's right." Monty's mother sounded vehement. "I knew when you turned eighteen, you would gain your inherited powers. Your father couldn't have you being stronger than him, so he tried to kill you. It took me a few weeks to figure out it was him, and I'm sorry you suffered so terribly. I stayed for you. I stayed *with* you. His powers of hatred, of darkness, were horrifying. But light and love are real. I sent for Bathilde." His mom smiled at her. "I love that you chose the name Lucille Ball when you came back to us. So Hollywood!"

Bathilde leaned in and hugged her. "I've missed you, my friend. Now. Where do you think Monty senior put the moon?"

"Wait—Is my name Tucker or Monty?" Monty asked.

"Tucker," Sawyer and his mother said in unison.

"We named you after your father when you became a baby again. We gave up our lives. Now. Let's find yours." She touched Monty's hand. "Let's split up."

They spent hours inside the house and out, looking for the moon-shaped glass bottle but couldn't. Outside, they wacked at the remaining balls dangling from the trees, and Monty even climbed several to remove barely visible blue bottles with mysterious notes inside.

Some were frightening. Monty's father had written curses on long-forgotten enemies and kept wishing harm to his son. He'd even written a curse to break up Monty and his ex-lover, Luke.

As they removed each bottle and ball, dark skies swirled overhead.

Suddenly, Monty turned to him. "It's in my old bedroom. Mom, I need the hammer."

Bathilde ran behind Monty and Sawyer. As they got to the bedroom, Monty was like a wild man, tearing the place apart. He pushed aside the bed, and the room turned black. The lights wouldn't work, and a foul stench invaded the space.

"It's here, I know it." Monty was on his knees, tears streaking down his face. "That smell, that horrible smell, this was what I lived with for months."

Sawyer became paralyzed. He couldn't move from where he was standing.

"What's happening?" Monty crawled to him, but nothing would shift Sawyer's frozen form.

Monty's mother came in with a hammer and flashlights. In

the flickering beam, Monty tapped the wooden floors until one board sounded hollow.

"Don't!" Bathilde suddenly screamed. She dropped on the floor beside Monty, and her hands became claw-like as she fought him for the hammer. "Don't take him away from me! If you kill the moon, you kill me. I can't be alone. Don't send me away! *Please!*"

Monty fought her off. She wailed and shrieked as he pried the floorboard up and pulled out the beautiful but deadly glass moon.

"Sorry, Bathilde. Love comes first!"

"No!" Bathilde screamed as Monty smashed the moon with the hammer, beating it again and again.

The house seemed to roar in approval. A deep, thundering sound emerged from the very foundation, everything shaking as though it had been hit by an earthquake.

Then everything went quiet. All that remained was a faint, smoky smell, and light flooded the room — beautiful, glorious, bright yellow light.

"Can you move?" Monty turned to Sawyer.

"Watch me."

Sawyer ran to him, and they collapsed into each other, Monty's mother wrapping her arms around them.

CHAPTER EIGHT

Thanksgiving

Monty couldn't remember ever being this happy. The past few days had gone by in a whirlwind. Monty, his mother, Sawyer, and his newly arrived Grammy spent their time cleaning up the house. Clearing it of any signs of blue glass, not to mention bad juju.

"I missed you, Grammy," Monty told her more than once.

She never changed, never seemed to grow old and grumpy. She went to work scrubbing the floors from one end to the other with saltwater mixed with a few drops of juniper oil. Monty had no idea where she got her energy, but she then set her focus on the windows and door handles.

She was thrilled to see Sawyer and didn't seem surprised to hear that Bathilde had tried to stop Monty from, er, killing the moon.

"She's a complicated creature that one," his grandmother said as she assembled the ingredients she needed to prepare pickles in gelatin and her crazy Coke salad.

"You seemed to get along well with her when you helped her save my life," Monty pointed out as he shelled fresh peas into a bowl in the kitchen.

"Of course, I did. But she's a boo hag. Unpredictable."

"What happens now? Is she dead?" Monty worried about that. He'd grown to love her and would miss her dearly, even though she'd tried to stop him from bringing Sawyer back to full life.

"Of course not. She's a ghost!" When Monty just looked at her, she tore open a box of black cherry flavored jello for her salad and shook the contents into a mixing bowl. "She will wait in the ether for the next soul who needs her." She tapped the box against the bowl lip and gave him a thoughtful look. "If you and Sawyer ever have children, she could be called upon to be a guardian spirit."

"Children! I never thought about that!"

"I did." Sawyer came up and put his arms around them. "But I'm in no hurry. How about you?" He nuzzled Monty's cheek.

"No. I want to get through Thanksgiving without any drama." Monty popped a pea into Sawyer's mouth.

He returned his focus to the task at hand. The turkey was in the oven, and the cornbread dressing would go in next. They'd made cheese straws for snacks as well as deviled eggs and two types of pickles. The dough for the honey buttermilk biscuits was resting in a pan before being baked. And the vegetables were all in varying stages of being cooked.

Monty had never invited company to any meal in the house, let alone an important family holiday. He couldn't even remember the last time he and his parents had celebrated anything here. In fact, the previous Thanksgiving, Monty had taken his mom to a Jewish deli for their meal while his father went on some mysterious expedition, which resulted in more weird religious relics. Christmas had been Chinese takeout.

Very depressing.

Not this year. Monty had a lot to be thankful for. Though he, his mom, and Grammy were scheduled to move into Sawyer's house over the weekend, they were leaving their old family home in a clean, fresh state for its next owners. Their plan was to sell the house and expand the cheese business.

We all need a new start. Monty felt his emotion welling up, and it was hard. Snatches of the last moments of his life before his father "killed" Sawyer kept coming back. He knew one day he wanted to go back to the barn in South Carolina, where his father had caught them. He wanted to go back and try to remember it all. Right now, the snatches of memories were enough. Painful and grim, there would be time enough to remember everything that had happened.

Today was a time of gratitude.

Monty had invited his former top salesman, Laurent, to celebrate the festive holiday with them. He arrived with his dog, Bella, who loped into the house and ran straight to Monty's old bedroom, lifted his leg, and peed on the spot where the moon had been buried.

Grammy crowed. "That's the spirit. That's a good sign when a dog's not afraid of some old voodoo magic."

"Voodoo?" Laurent's eyebrows flew up toward his hairline.

"She's joking," Monty's mom assured him. "She's got a strange sense of humor."

Grammy looked pissed but said nothing. Every family had its secrets. Some more than others.

Monty had so many questions about his past, but any he asked gave him responses that left him feeling queasy. He was glad his dad was somewhere safe, somewhere . . . secure, where he couldn't wield his cruelty over anybody, especially his family. He really was like two people. Doting family man running a cheese shop, and crazy voodoo guy with obsessive-compulsive disorder and a worsening religious mania on top of it all.

Monty gave Laurent a hug, surprised to see who he'd brought as his guest. It was one of Monty's old friends, Leanne, who'd dropped out of sight around the time Laurent had.

"He said he was bringing a guest, but I never thought it

would be you!" Monty hugged Leanne hard. "When did this happen?"

"I read his Instagram posts, and we started exchanging private messages. A few weeks ago, I told him to come home. I know he's in a fragile state, but it's all good. Life is good. We'll figure it out together." She hugged Monty hard.

Leanne and Sawyer seemed to hit it off immediately, which warmed Monty's heart.

They'd set up the dining table outside, and it had never looked so lovely. Without the oppressive glass balls and bottles, the backyard looked like a vision out of *Martha Stewart Living*.

Monty's mother had brought out her favorite linens. The tabletop décor consisted of fresh greens, a few fallen maple leaves gathered from around the neighborhood, baby pumpkins and squashes, and pumpkin spice-scented votive candles in glasses.

Everybody admired the table as they enjoyed a glass of the wine Sawyer had brought. Monty knew it must have cost a fortune and knew they'd have to talk about money one day. Had Sawyer's family been wealthy?

Curiosity got the better of him, so he asked, "What happened to your family?"

"They were worse than your father, but at least they didn't try to kill me. I came to live with your family when they disowned me. That's how we met and fell in love. Don't worry, in time, it will all come back to you," was all he would say.

Monty could not have loved him more as he watched Sawyer squatting on the ground, rubbing Bella's belly.

Everybody loved the nibbles, and they snacked as Bella gobbled a small bowl of pieces of turkey, minus its skin, on the ground beside them.

The day was glorious. Cool and mild with a pale yolk sun poking out of the sky.

Bella lay on the ground, lazily watching a falling leaf.

"We're getting fall finally," Monty said. "Usually we go from summer straight to winter. I love this time of year."

They toasted each other's health and future good fortune.

"Hey," Laurent suddenly said, "I heard the news on the way over here that an orderly from this assisted living facility was arrested for killing some guys on your street." He flicked through his cell phone.

Monty exchanged an anguished glance with Sawyer. When Laurent turned the phone around so they could see the photo of the man. Monty was shocked to see it was Tommy de Anzo.

What the hell? He was an orderly at my dad's facility? Holy heck. That means Dad is somehow able to control people into doing his bidding. Grammy said he had great and terrible powers at one point. But until Mom said he'd been a voodoo king, I had no idea how strong he was.

Laurent went on. "Only thing is, they say his prints don't match the earlier assaults. Just the last one, so they're still looking for the guy who did it. There's still a serial killer out there!" Laurent focused his attention on the food Monty's mother started bringing to the table.

Monty followed her back into the kitchen to help, Sawyer hot on his heels.

"Have you checked on Dad? he asked her.

"I'm going to call now. Please don't worry. They've got him locked up." She patted his shoulder.

"Mom, Tommy de Anzo posed as a cheese vendor and came into the shop. Now he turns out to be the orderly that took Dad out of that place and let him run crazy!"

His mother's face paled. "Get everything on the table. I'll check on him. Did you take the pecan pie out of the oven?" For the first time in days, she seemed agitated and flustered.

"I got it, don't worry. It's cooling on the benchtop," Sawyer said, his voice calm. "Come on, babe, let's get everything out on the table."

Several minutes later, with everybody helping themselves to the magnificent spread outside, Monty's mother came out, cell phone in hand.

"I just spoke to your dad, and he's sorry he can't be here. He wishes everyone a very Happy Thanksgiving." She gave Monty a wink.

He wished he could feel her sense of relief, but he didn't.

The meal went well, but he couldn't shake the feeling of doom, even as he ate his favorite dessert, cranberry upside-down cake with extra whipped cream. He ate a slice of the bourbon pecan pie and had just started to relax when Laurent and Leanne said they had to leave.

"I hate to admit it, but Rima invited us to dinner." Laurent avoided Monty's gaze.

Monty couldn't believe it.

"I know she and her mom haven't been good to you, but she's my friend."

Monty said nothing. He had plans to deal with Rima. Plans she wouldn't like. He felt wounded that Laurent had come here and not told him he was still close to Rima.

Leanne hugged Monty goodbye. "Sorry," she whispered in his ear, "I knew he should have told you sooner."

They left without taking any leftovers, except scraps of turkey for Bella and few stray cheese straws.

"Rima's obsessed with these," Laurent said.

When they left, Monty and Sawyer took the remnants of their meal to the kitchen, cleaning up while their womenfolk took naps. It was around five o'clock, and the sky grew dark as Monty stacked the dishwasher.

"Days are getting shorter," he said as a cloud seemed to move over the house.

"No. Something's up." Sawyer glanced up from the wine glass he'd washed by hand and was now carefully drying. "Trouble, babe." He put down the glass on the sideboard, and with an odd look on his face, turned and walked toward the front door.

"Don't! Let me call the police!" Monty yelled.

But Sawyer kept moving. Suddenly he turned. "I love you. Never forget that."

Monty screamed for his mother and grandmother. They came running, but by the time they arrived, Sawyer had left the house. The front door was open, and there was no trace of him.

"I'm calling the police," Monty said.

The 9-1-1 operator answered immediately. "9-1-1. What is your emergency?" she asked.

"There's, um, suspicious activity on my street," he said, glancing from left to right then back again. Down the end of the block, he saw it. A black cape. A shrill scream pierced the quiet.

"Oh, my God." Grammy ran down toward the scene.

"No!" Monty ran after her. The 9-1-1 operator gave him instructions, but he couldn't keep up with them. "I have to go." He ended the call and raced to catch his grandmother, and came to the end of the street. The man in the black cape turned.

"Oh no!" Monty saw Laurent, dead on the ground, Leanne across the road holding Bella in her arms.

Sawyer lay beside Laurent, injured but alive.

The man in the black cape sneered at Monty. "I think I always hated you."

"I think I always knew that . . . Dad."

His father came at him with his big, gleaming knife, but out of nowhere, shots rang out. Monty looked. It was Grammy with the family shotgun. She'd blown two holes in his father's chest. He flew back and fell onto the street, laughing then coughing and finally, nothing.

"He was my son, but I should have done it a long time

ago." She looked triumphant. "I did it. I really did it. Grammy get your gun!"

Monty stared at her. He wished he could have felt grief, or shock, or something, but Sawyer was on his feet now, and Monty held him hard.

"I'm okay," he said, "I'm okay."

Sawyer had known there would be a showdown and wondered why the old man had killed Laurent. He and Monty figured Monty senior was angry that Laurent and Monty had remained friends.

Leanne told the police the old man had been waiting at their car for them, and they ran.

"We ran and ran," she said. "I had no idea, but Larry was terrified of that old guy. And then he had the knife, and he killed him."

The police said that Monty's dad had been the serial killer. His prints matched the earlier attacks.

Leanne and Bella went home to her mom's in Carmel, and Monty, his grandmother, and his mother moved in with Sawyer that night.

"That house, the juju just won't let go of us," Grammy said.

Perhaps she was right.

Sawyer made up beds for the women in the rooms they picked out, and he checked all the door and window locks to make sure they were safe. He felt nothing but relief that the old man was gone. He knew his loved ones were going to be okay because he was protected, and so were they. They were no longer at the mercy of his vicious and selfish power.

He found Monty waiting for him in bed and wished they hadn't lost so many good years. *Salad Days are Here Again!*

We won't waste our time. I'm here. He's here. And we love each other. That's all that matters.

"Alexa, play our song," Monty called out to the electronic gizmo that vibrated with a blue light then played *Let's Spend the Night Together.*

"You're remembering!" Sawyer slid into the sheets beside him.

"I remember you started to fuck me to this song. I was a virgin." He paused. "We were in the barn when my father came in. Oh!" His mouth dropped open.

"We both were." Sawyer lay beside him, listening to the Rolling Stones preaching utter naughtiness.

"Oh, my God. He wasn't alone. Freddie Piano was with him." Monty's face went slack. "He helped my father hurt us."

"He's been making up for it ever since."

Monty reached for him. "We belong to each other."

"Now, more than ever." Sawyer let his lover strip him of his clothes. They lost themselves in their embrace, their sighs given up to the night.

Sawyer took his time, touching, tasting Monty's skin. He could never get enough of him.

"You take too long." Monty pushed Sawyer away from him and put him on his back. His eyes gleamed as he took Sawyer's cock into his mouth and sucked him with abandon. His eyes closed with pleasure.

Sawyer loved watching the way Monty took his time, moving his mouth up and down, releasing Sawyer's length with a pop, then devouring it again.

Monty glanced at him, his eyes filled with lust. "I can't take much more. Gotta have you. Now."

Sawyer nodded, mute with desire. He relaxed his body more though his cock was rigid. Monty mounted him, hovering as he rubbed his ass against Sawyer's shaft. At one point, Sawyer's cock tip rubbed against Monty's tailbone, making Monty moan. It took everything in Sawyer not to throw his lover on his back and stick it into him. They had to learn to savor things. They had to learn to take their time.

He grabbed Monty's bouncing length, holding it in his possessive grip. Monty slowly lowered himself onto Sawyer, moving his hips slowly until he had Sawyer buried in him all the way.

Sawyer gripped Monty's left hip, using his right hand to cuff and pull on his cock. They rocked against one another, their mouths crushing together until they came within seconds of one another.

When it was all over, sweet, yet still not satisfying enough, Sawyer gazed into Monty's eyes. "What song should we play to make love all night?"

"I don't care." Monty touched his face with reverent fingers. "As long as the song never ends and we come together again. And again."

Sawyer kissed him. "Sounds good to me. Alexa, play *Happy Together*."

Monty laughed as the song began. "Put it on repeat."

Alexa said something, but Sawyer lost interest in anything but his man and the song. He hoped it would play on forever.

Because they had been. Then. And now. Happy together.

Monty's Grammy's Southern Cheese Straws

Ingredients:
- 1 teaspoon kosher or sea salt
- 1/4 teaspoon cayenne pepper
- 1/4 teaspoon smoked paprika
- 1/2 pound sharp cheddar, room temperature
- 1/2 cup (1 stick) butter, room temperature

Preparation:

1. Heat oven to 375 degrees. Grate cheese.

2. In a food processor, pulse dry ingredients until combined, then add cheese and butter. Process until dough becomes smooth and has the texture of Play-Doh. Alternately, make the dough in a stand mixer by creaming cheese and butter until smooth. Then combine dry ingredients in a bowl and combine with butter mixture at low speed until smooth.

3. Shape the dough into a cylinder, wrap with plastic wrap or parchment and allow to rest for 20 minutes. Or store in the refrigerator until ready to bake.

4. Bring dough to room temperature and pack it into a cookie press fitted with a star disk. Pipe long ribbons of dough across the baking sheet lined with parchment paper or a silicone mat, about an inch apart. Then cut into six-inch lengths. Repeat with remaining dough. Dough may also be hand-rolled into long ropes and cut to size or shaped into a cylinder and sliced into rounds and baked.

5. Bake for about 13 minutes or until the edges just begin to brown. Store between sheets of parchment or waxed paper in an airtight container. Will keep for up to three weeks.

ABOUT THE AUTHOR

A.J. Llewellyn is the author of over 300 M/M romance novels. She was born in Australia, and lives in Los Angeles. An early obsession with Robinson Crusoe led to a lifelong love affair with islands, particularly Hawaii and Easter Island.

Being marooned once on Wedding Cake Island in Australia cured her of a passion for fishing but led to a plotline for a novel. A.J.'s friends live in fear because even the smallest details of their lives usually wind up in her stories. A.J. has a desire to sing, paint, draw, juggle, work for the FBI, walk a tightrope with an elephant, be a chess champion, a steeplejack, master chef, a knitter and crochet queen, and a world-class surfer. She can't do any of these things, so she writes about them instead.

A.J. I started life as a journalist and boxing columnist, and still enjoys interrogating, er, interviewing people to find out what makes them tick.

www.ingramcontent.com/pod-product-compliance
Lightning Source LLC
Chambersburg PA
CBHW060626130626
46555CB00002B/685